NEIL MUST DIE

Neil Must Die

When death is not of the body...
but of the soul...

Kaberi Chatterjee

Cover design: Samit Chanda
Cover model: Debarati Roy
Model photograph: Debanjana Roy
Author photograph: Aniruddha Chatterjee

Order this book online at www.trafford.com
or email orders@trafford.com

Most Trafford titles are also available at major online book retailers.

Printed in Victoria, BC, Canada.

ISBN: 978-1-4269-2878-9

*Our mission is to efficiently provide the world's finest, most comprehensive book publishing
service, enabling every author to experience success. To find out how to publish your book, your
way, and have it available worldwide, visit us online at www.trafford.com*

Trafford rev. 3/08/2010

 www.trafford.com

North America & international
toll-free: 1 888 232 4444 (USA & Canada)
phone: 250 383 6864 ♦ fax: 812 355 4082

Other book written by the author:
Titir and other Tales

For my progeny…

'I am ready to meet my Maker. Whether my Maker is prepared for the great ordeal of meeting me is another matter.' — Winston Churchill

Preface

I wrote *Neil Must Die* in three weeks.

Then the novel gathered dust for 10 years. A few people read it — to be precise, about two or three — liked it and I was happy. Publishing it really never crossed my mind.

I started writing it in June, 2000, after a camping trip to a beautiful place called Hodolchua, in Purulia district, West Bengal, India. The beauty of the place inspired me to write. Hodolchua features right at the end.

I wrote the novel for two hours before dawn, just before my husband and three-year-old son woke up — with a pen on papers — before the sundries of the daybreak snatched me off from my world of Neil and Tuli. It's as if Neil and Tuli existed in my life. They were real. I was simply penning down whatever happened to their lives. I, often, did not know what would really happen to them. I still think they existed, somewhere...

I cried when sad things happened to Neil and Tuli. So much, that I dampened the paper I was writing on and had to get a new sheet. It was as if I was watching their lives unfold, not creating their characters and writing their story.

No, they really did not exist. Glimpses of the characters in this novel may be found in everyday lives of everybody. And most people may find I wrote about them. But fact is that, I wrote about myself and people around me I loved. Our pains and pleasures of growing up. Our loss of true self-identity and shocking revelations. Our realization of the reality and learning to live with it. And then, escaping from the reality...

It is often I come across a quiz: What would you do if this was your last day on earth?

You can guess what I'd like to answer: I would run away.

Neil is lucky. He went in circles, but escaped. Because he existed at an age when one could get lost. Now you cannot. Communication will catch up with you.

If you know, please tell me one place where technology will not be able to catch me. I want to escape!

By the end of the eighth year of its hibernation, I reluctantly showed extracts of *Neil Must Die* to my editor, in the newspaper where I was working. He read it and said: You write such good English, why do you make mistakes in your headlines?

That was the best review I have of this novel so far. Though he wanted to emphasize on my mistakes in the headlines, I choose to embrace the first part of his comment.

People who read my manuscript: My friends Krishnadi, Titli and Sylvia, my husband and my brother's fiancé, Raka.

People who didn't read my manuscript:

My mom: Thinks it's too long!

My dad: I am too embarrassed to show him for the adult contents…

My sister: My greatest critic, yet she's up to her neck in chores running after her two toddlers.

My brother: 'Yeah, yeah, I'll read it…!'

Acknowledgements

My husband is a very impatient man and cannot read anything for long. Not even newspapers. He was my first reader. I held his attention for more than three hours at a stretch while reading out my book to him and he still says it was not a book he read, it was a movie he watched. I am grateful to him for his attention.

My teenage son: Who represented the growing years. Impatient, yearning for affection, yet independent, resenting attention. He read snatches and was interested. It mattered.

Parna: Who agreed to smile for the cover without a hint of hesitation.

Krishnadi: My ever-widening plateau of freedom and self-identity.

Titli: My sudden-found friend, philosopher and guide and the editor of this novel.

My brother: His lost-and-found-identity track record made my job easier. Only he would understand this.

And last but not the least, my parents: I built my base on their round-the-clock support.

CATHY

CHAPTER 1

Bhuntar, Himalayas, India, October 9, 1996

Neil looked out of the glass panels of his balcony door. He was naked. A burnt out cigarette stuck lifelessly to the fingers on his left hand. It had marijuana into its emptied-out cylinder. His head felt good.

The snow-peaked mountains posted outside were pink, bathing in the glow of the dawn. The hilly stretch of road leading out from the hotel he was staying at, wound behind a camouflage of pine trees and thorny bushes — into nowhere. The girl he was sleeping with that night, ushered herself discreetly through the path; inconspicuously hiding herself in a shabby shawl.

A faint rhythm of *Mahalaya* [1] filtered into his ears from somewhere. The divine sonata was reaching its finale and had ascended towards an orgasm of nostalgia.

Neil tossed the burnt out cigarette hard onto the floor. The 23-year-old youth was far away from home.

He was feeling uneasy. He walked towards the bed and put on his basics. The girl had charged five hundred bucks. Worth giving! Neil looked into his wallet. He had enough.

His bus was at eight-thirty a.m. It was only five. He had plenty of time. He plopped onto the bed.

It had been a tough day. First, there was a breakdown of the bus he had taken from Delhi. Two hours of a relentlessly hot countryside at mid-afternoon. There were squealing babies and grumbling passengers, for the air-conditioning in the bus too was off. However, they could do nothing except curse the ever-apologizing bus driver and conductor. Neil sat still for the two hours, except taking off twice to smoke. He never felt perturbed.

He had gone through other merciless agonies.

Then the girl came in late. After attending two other customers. Then she had to take a bath. She said she was finicky about that.

"Come on," Neil had laughed. "You are not going through some kind of a prayer session."

"No *babuji* [2], we always take a bath after attending each customer. This baboon was an arsehole. He didn't like what I did to him. So he threw me out halfway. I could have taken a bath in his bathroom."

"How many customers can you fit in?"

"About three, sometimes four."

Neil was suddenly curious. He never usually was. But her soft, tribal looks provoked his curiosity. She was barely in her late teens. With garish make-up she tried to hide both her age and her naiveté.

"Where do you live?" he asked.

"Here, down the hill"

Neil knew that for the people living in the hills 'here' meant quite a few kilometers off.

He was tempted to ask her name, but restrained himself. Half of these people had made-up ones. And moreover he didn't want to put her on guard.

The girl took a bath and slathered herself extravagantly with Neil's after-shave. Then, adeptly, she put on the hotel's piped music and drew the curtains. She switched off all the lights barring the night lamp and began swinging to the tune, professionally taking off her clothes one by one…

CHAPTER 2

The bus left the hotel at sharp at eight-thirty. Sometimes punctuality in this country surprised Neil. He was prepared for a breakdown, a lackadaisical driver or late passengers. But it was apparent that the hills had their own set of rules. People dissected themselves mentally from the core of the country's red-tapism.

He did not get a window seat. He loved the mountains and wanted to switch off all connections with reality once he was with the Himalayas.

The vehicle was barely a 20-seater. It had tinted windows — an impression given to passengers that the bus was a luxury one. In reality, the seats were far from comfortable. There was very little leg-room and the backrest was too upright. Most tourists had no options, for on a short stretch like his, investing on luxury transport was the last thing on a bus-owner's mind.

A clamor of children came from the rear. Without glancing behind Neil knew they were from a bunch from a middle-class Bengali family. Where these people get all that money to travel, he had often wondered. When all they could afford at best were government jobs, Bengali-medium schooling for their children and packets of eccentric looking saris during the *Durga puja* [3].

He didn't turn back. He knew what they would be like. He had seen scores of them in his own family. The women had big bosoms that had turned bigger with over-feeding their children with breast-milk and fat strings tied round their left arms where a barrage of small metal cubes hung. They were called *madulis* [4] and were supposed to change fate. They mostly wore synthetic saris, the best they thought for rough travelling, and *bindis* [5]. There ended their make-up. Their daughters wore lacy dresses with colored hair clips, at best; beads, and a disparaging touch of colorful *bindis* on their foreheads. Their sons wore shirts and short pants with shoes and socks for that final dressed-up look. Their husbands wore the same kind of terry-cotton shirts and black pants and a gamut of rings fitted with stones, on their fingers — all which were supposed to change their fates.

Neil thought of trying out one. He had a fate he definitely wanted to change.

CHAPTER 3

Bhuntar. Beneath the mammoth range of the Himalayas this town was just a dot. But it was a devouring spot for mountain-hungry travelers. For this was the access to India's most daunting trek routes.

In India there were two classes of people — one made money and had money. The other class never made money but *spent* money. It was the second pedigree that had Indian Railways always on the wheels. These people loved to travel around — for this part of the Asian peninsula had the most lavish number of temples and historical edifices, probably in the entire continent — rivers and exotic caves, excavations and artificial water parks. Not to mention the enveloping range of the fantastic intoxication called the Himalayas.

The mountain range had its beauty specified in layers — soft and green in places and a bursting frenzy of color in others. Elsewhere, it was grim, dusty, thorny and unfriendly with sharp edges sliced off over hanging cliffs. However, they all tapered towards the heaven in white snow-capped finales.

Neil never belonged to any of the categories. He worked on simple logic. And visiting the mountains right now was his necessity.

His father and grandfather had made shelves of money through a business of gold and leather. Before that, his ancestors were serving the loyal coterie of the British regime. Their imposing kingdom in central Calcutta, thanks to the kindness of their patrons, was a vast two-storied edifice more than a hundred years old. It housed three families — Neil's, consisting of his elder brother, mother and father, who were the crux of the whole unit; and his two uncles with their four children. They were jointly united under a single business and a single kitchen.

The typical traditional Bengali domain had a square courtyard in the centre, which opened up to the sky. Ornate railings and baroque arcades with colored glass panes, bordering a wide balcony on the first floor, ran around the courtyard. The square courtyard terminated in an elaborately ornamented and elevated platform with pillars and baroque arches, called the *thakurdalan* [6]; essentially kept empty and holy for worshipping the Goddess *Durga* once a year during autumn. This celebration was the annual and final one of the Bengalis and marked the advent of peace and harmony in their land. Possessing a *thakurdalan* was the ultimate status quo.

The carpet area of the balcony on the first floor was a labyrinth of black and white marble and thanks to the strictures of the house, spotless. More than eight rooms in each floor overlooked the balcony, and in turn, the courtyard.

Each bedroom had two windows and two doors; a folding glass-panel aligned with a wide wooden one with Venetian blinds. The building touched the apical in an enormous terrace, a weird one in layers, each layer representing the room below it. Bedrooms had high ceilings and kitchens had low. The dining room touched a medium height.

Central Calcutta had a trait. It was considered the oldest and the most cultured face of the megalopolis — if not, of the country. To exemplify its worth, the spot was lined by shanty bookstalls that housed a multitudinous collection of literature from all over the globe. They came in inconspicuous covers and from hidden and dusty shelves. The booksellers seldom knew the real worth of their books and sold them at dirt-cheap rates. A real book-lover cognized the precise stall and headed for it.

The large extent of the haughty locale housed another of the city's features — sweets. Marvelous sweets inside not-so-convincing glass cabinets attracted both customers and flies, alike. And newly sprung up smaller shops dwelling in this reputation paved a distinct career-path for the unemployed youth in this part of the city. Towards the 21st century, however, along with other industries, Bengalis were losing out on the sweet-monopoly too. For a distinct clan from the west, Rajasthan, off-handedly referred to as Marwaris, pushed the Bengalis out of the monopoly, with their more coveted *mithais* [7] smeared with extra *ghee* [8] and dry fruits.

Neil had graduated from the most prestigious college of the city, situated predictably, in this locale. He mastered the most coveted language of India, English, and had his ineptly educated father and uncles raving about this 'golden boy'. Only the 'golden boy' in concern knew that a degree in English would do nothing for a future in the city. Two decades of Marxism in the state might have done a few wonders for the rural restitution and the city's safety and security, but along with industries nose-diving into non-existence, un-employment had reached a point of plethora and Neil knew he could be no exception.

But his father had money; millions of colored ones, which he bestowed on his favorite son as pocket money. Neil bought a computer with his savings and transformed a deserted, creaky, almost a haunted dump-room at the terrace into a private study. He covered the brick-bearing walls and ceiling with very exclusive wallpaper and set the floor in linoleum tiles. All this cost money and that was not his own. He knew he had to return it one day to his father.

He needn't have actually.

His room led out onto the wide expanse of the terrace that overlooked the bustle below, and smelt sweet and polluted. Trams, bullock carts, shaky and speedy aluminum buses, smoke-spewing taxis, hand-pulled rickshaws, along with, with the result of a recent open-market strategy of the government, foreign-India collaborated vehicles like Benz, Suzuki, Daewoo and Indian Maruti, plied the streets. They jostled with each other in narrow roadways, most of the time resulting in periods of honking and endless traffic congestion.

The evenings were a little different, barring the huge psychedelic advertisements screaming out their products atop houses and a line-up of gory looking prostitutes of all ages, leaning on the footpath railings. For, along with the best books, the best gold and the best sweets, central Calcutta also housed the best girls.

Very impressive part of the country. But Neil had lived there from birth and it held no more fascination, at worse a little irritation. The terrace gave him barely a niche in the claustrophobic arena. But he placed the computer near the window opening onto the terrace. He could view an expanse of the white sky. He was satisfied. In India, the sky remains primarily white during greater part of the year due to excessive sunlight and pollution.

He was satisfied by very few things. Sexy girls were one of them. And the foreigner girl who brushed through his legs quite unabashedly right now for the window seat next to him, seemed to be one.

CHAPTER 4

She was white; a skin color fetching good money in this country. She was in jeans and a mauve pullover. Her golden hair was short up to her neck. Her rucksack was on her lap and her eyes were closed.

Neil decided to stare at her. He leant back his head and examined her face first. She had light colored eyebrows, and obviously had a set of light colored eyes. He hadn't noticed them when she had sat down. He wondered what colors they could be. Light brown? Aquamarine blue? Green or simply grey? Her lips were burnt red. Her cheeks were speckled and so was her nose. She must have been on the road for some time. Those were sunspots.

Her neck was long and slim. The way he had wanted all Indian girls to have theirs. She was asleep and her hands fell off unguardedly. Her breasts were small from what Neil could discern beneath the pullover.

"Do you mind?!" Neil jumped at the words and looked up. Her eyes were open and they were a shocking black! Obviously she had caught Neil examining her valued anatomy and hailing from a mentally more uninhibited country, showed no unnecessary shame in possessing them, the way an Indian girl would.

Neil adjusted his sitting position, smirked a little and looked away.

The bus roared its engine. The conductor gave signals for it to take off. The small vehicle waddled its way up the busy street into the mountains for a small village called Manikaran. Neil's fourteen-kilometer trek on foot up to a village called Pulga would begin from there.

He turned to his side. The girl was up and looked distantly through the open window. The cool wind disheveled her hair completely.

"Hi!" Neil extended his hand, "I'm Neil."

"I am not interested," she turned halfway and rudely cut in. She obviously thought him to be another street-side Romeo that probably flocked through her journey through India.

Neil grinned and pulled back his hand. "Oh hi, Miss Not-interested. Er… you can keep your bag up there, you know. That way I can view your legs better."!

A slap! Oh my God! This time a tight slap was surely due. He held his breath.

The girl turned to him. Her face was stern, her black eyes cold against her whitish features. Then she burst into a smile and turned away to look out of the window.

On second thoughts she plopped her heavy rucksack on Neil's legs. "I'm Cathy."

Neil said "Ouch!" and then lifted the bag to keep it on the narrow shelf running above the seats. "What do you carry? Bricks? To hit all Indian men?" he said after brushing his hands off imaginary dirt, the way one does after a job well done.

He sat down beside her and took out a packet of chewing gums from his pocket.

"Friends?" he said and extended one strip to her.

"Not so fast." She took the packet, tore out one and put it in her mouth.

She chewed on it and contorted her mouth. "Yikes, it's horrible!"

"Hey, this is from your lands." Neil popped one into his mouth.

Cathy turned to him, "Where are you off to?"

"Pulga. I love treks."

"Oh my God!" gasped Cathy.

"What happened?"

"Aren't there any more trek routes out there? I want to change my route."

Neil grinned wickedly. "Somebody up there loves me!" he hummed and laughed aloud.

Cathy smirked lightly. She extended her legs underneath the seat in front of her and leant back. "Okay, for the time being, can you leave me alone?"

"Oh sure," said Neil and smiled.

"Good," said Cathy and closed her eyes.

Neil leant back and began tunelessly humming the movie song that was being played in the bus.

His voice reached an octave when Cathy opened her eyes. "Okay, okay, we'll talk."

Neil stopped singing. "Oh, really?"

"Anything to make you stop singing."

" Oh! Sorry. Did I disturb you?"

"No, no, of course not. You were just a note worse than the bus engine."

"Ha! Ha! You're joking!"

"Joking?" Cathy turned to him, "I'm serious. You're good. It's just that I can't take such wonderful music."

"Where are you from?" Neil cut in.

She looked away. "None of your business." She looked out of the window and said, "Sweden."

"You speak English very well."

"I am an American. My husband is working for a Swedish company."

"Your husband…?" Neil turned to her looking sorrowful.

"Oh, yes! Big and kicking! He's Swedish, you know and his hobby is bull-fighting."

"Oh mah Gawd!" Neil jumped an imaginary inch away. Then remembering something he said, "Bull-fighting is from Spain, isn't it?"

"So what? It's contagious. Now every country in Europe is picking it up."

Neil fell silent. Then turned to her and said, "You're not lying, are you? I mean… you don't look married…"

She quickly groped around her handbag and took out a photograph from inside it. She handed it to him, "Isn't he cute?"

A grotesque pair of eyes beneath a bushy, threatening set of eyebrows, a big nose and a large mouth set in a wide-jawed face with crew-cut hair, stared at him. Neil took the snap and quickly gave it back to Cathy.

"Yeah!" he smiled pathetically and raised his eyebrows.

"That's not my husband. That's my boyfriend," said Cathy. "Here's my husband."

She handed him a lesser intimidating photograph. The man seemed to be a soberly dressed professor in his early thirties, complete with glasses and a thin moustache. He handed back the photo.

"You are an interesting character."

Cathy smiled pleasingly and nodded her head.

"And what are they doing now? Shopping together for you?" he asked smilingly.

Cathy smiled, "I've ditched my boyfriend before coming to India."

"Oh, good! So your husband won, right?"

Cathy turned to him. "Enough talking about me. Now tell me about yourself. Where are you from?"

"Me?" Neil turned slightly defensive. "I am from Calcutta."

"Bengali?"

He nodded.

"You speak English very well, too," she smiled.

A very discreetly camouflaged anger seeped out from his next words.

"We've had two hundred years of formal training, you see!"

"Two hundred...?" Cathy initially looked perplexed. Then understanding the meaning of his words, she smiled sympathetically. "You're still angry with the British?" She knew the Indian history slightly. India had been under a painful British colonization for over 200 years until it was freed very recently.

Neil turned away and somberly nodded his head in the negative. Then smiled and looked at her, "If it wasn't for them, we would have still been in the dark ages."

"Ha! Ha!" smiled Cathy teasingly. "So you do admit defeat?"

Neil suddenly turned away and turned serious. "Can we change the topic?" There was a distinct volcano in his voice. A blurred picture of a young man rolling down the stairs of his house, blood getting smeared on the steps and two victorious policemen marching down after the body with revolvers, shaped and vanished from his mind's eye... It perhaps happened when Neil was very young. Or perhaps he overheard his elders talking about it until the impression formed in colored pictures inside his mind's eye. He didn't know. He never wanted to find out.

They both fell silent for a while.

Then she spoke. "Who do you have in your family?"

Neil sighed slightly and looked at her, "My wife and seven children."

"WHAT...?!!" Cathy gasped!

Neil looked sorrowful and said, "Yeah, not planned, you see, accidents."

"You're joking," Cathy said in a definite tone.

"Yes," Neil smiled, "the wife part."

"Wha...! You..." Cathy burst out smiling. "You're impossible! How did you survive so long? Nobody beat you up?"

"Nope." Neil shook his head sincerely.

"Okay. So you're not interested in talking about yourself, right?"

Neil suddenly held her head and turned it towards the window. "See the mountains? We're way off them. We've just started to climb. We have two more hours to go."

He paused. Cathy turned to him. He smiled. "I'll not be able to escape."

She fell silent.

The bus was beginning to climb up-hill. The creamy roads through an ascending landscape with foothills all around green fields now began to look portentous. Mountains soon crammed up nearer on one side, while on the other side the green fields and landscape began to fall further and further down. River Parvati moved along, sometimes becoming a ribbon thrown down into the deep valley, sometimes a cool, swirling entertainer, jumping around their pathway. Their climb had begun. The bus roared its engine louder and began taking not-so-friendly turns at completely unprepared-for bends.

Cathy closed her eyes. It was obvious she decided not to ask him any more personal details.

Neil sensed that. He loomed over her and said, "With eyes closed you look beautiful."

She opened them and flinched away, "Do you mind?" She seemed to like that phrase very much.

"No I don't," Neil said. "Anything to keep you awake."

"But it looked like you didn't want to speak?"

"I *am* speaking."

"I mean ... about yourself."

"Okay." Neil sighed. "What do you want to know?"

"It's okay. I don't want to make you feel uncomfortable."

"I am very comfortable with you," he snuggled an inch closer.

"Hello…!" scolded Cathy.

He grinned. Then became a shade serious and said, "What do you want to know?"

"What do you do, for instance?"

"Me?" He pondered. "I ruin money." He laughed and then waved his hand, "Sorry!"

He turned somber for a while. He tried to frame his answer. A first-class college graduate running away from sickening jobs he didn't want to do? A computer-buffer?

Or a criminal with a track record of assisting in a murder and slipping through the fingers of law abetted by an influential mafia person?!

"I escape." He framed the answer and looked very happy with himself for doing so. He turned a smiling face to Cathy.

She looked nauseated. And turned away.

"Okay, I'll be honest with you." He decided to edit some of his track records. "I am a graduate looking for a job."

Cathy sighed. At last she managed a sensible answer from him. She nodded and asked off-handed, as if to keep the conversation going, "What do you specialize in?"

Neil sensed it. He turned grave. "Girls."

She looked at him stoically for a moment. Then asked, "Just the anatomy or an Ischemic heart too?"

Neil kept looking doleful. "Anatomy. I have yet to come across an Ischemic heart." He leant back and whisking a warm spice to his voice he added, "I'd love to."

She nodded, "Oh, yeah." She half-asked the question. She turned away and then half-turned. "You know, you should go a little slow on your specialized objects' nerves. You seem to be picking on them too much." She waved her hand in the air, "Just a friendly advice."

Neil jumped up and extended his hand, "Caught you. So we're friends?"

Cathy got startled. She was caught unawares. Then she shook the hand with a pungent expression. "You're disgusting!" She chewed on the words.

"Thanks," Neil smiled. "I'm flattered."

CHAPTER 5

The vehicle came to a halt at a village called Kasol. The conductor announced in Hindi. "The bus will stop here for 15 minutes. You can go to the bathrooms if you like," and alighted to get behind a tree for his own excretion.

Cathy turned to Neil and extended her hand, "May I?"

Neil stood up. "Of course." She squeezed herself out and glancing at her luggage once, alighted the bus and joined the chaotic family sitting behind them, lining for the toilet. Neil patted his pockets and took out his cigarettes. He disembarked and lighted one. Then steered himself behind a tree for a release.

A stall was selling tea. Neil ordered for a cup. Instantly the dark man in a soiled vest and grey pants poured out a steaming liquid that was boiling heavily in a sooty kettle, into a tiny earthen cup. Handing it to Neil he said, "Two rupees."

Neil took out a coin and exchanged it with the cup. The liquid was burning hot and sweet and smelt of an overdose of cheap tea-leaves and milk. But it felt good. He guessed it was the air. The growing chill in the weather made anything you ate or drank taste good. He sipped on the liquid and saw Cathy walking back, treading carefully on the slippery mud-path. She looked like a helpless child, who could slip and fall any moment. Neil thought of offering help. But something in him stopped him.

He remembered Tuli.

And *Katoa*.

And *Ajay river.* The intoxication of the boat-ride. The falling dusk and the slow pace of the boat, which had no intentions of ever returning to reality.

They were sitting on a bamboo seat outside the tegument of the boat facing the placid river. Tuli had shifted close to him and had laid her head on his shoulders. Oblivious to the boatman, who smoked a *bidi* [9] and sang a *bhatiali* [10] perching himself at the risky end of the boat, Tuli turned Neil's face and perched a kiss on his lips.

"The boatman can see."

"F++k the boatman," Tuli smiled and kissed him on his nose.

Then it began. Slowly. Sluggishly. At a leisurely pace. They held their lips lightly against each other's, testing their restraint, for what seemed hours. They let the fire rage inside them, magnetism overtake them completely. And then they kissed. With such severity that they both lost balance and fell right inside the tegument of the boat.

The spell snapped. They burst out laughing. Tuli struggled up and tugged at Neil's hand, his still head hanging in between two wooden planks meant to be seats. He was laughing. He wanted to lie down like that forever.

"*Babu*, anything happened?" The boatman's voice came from the rear.

"No," Neil scrambled up. "Do you have a match?" He stepped out and looked over the tegument and asked the boatman.

"Yes *babu*." He held out a matchbox over the low boat cover and took the liberty to ask a personal question. "Newly married?"

Neil pressed his mouth in a desire to laugh. He had faced that question before. "Yes."

Tuli giggled inside.

Neil stooped low, sat down on the bamboo seat and lit a cigarette. Tuli snuggled beside him. "Give me this one. You light another."

"You are getting quite addicted." Neil lighted another.

"Yah," Tuli gleamed. "Isn't it exciting? I want to try out grass." She wound her arm around his and took a deep drag from the burning roll, "Lets' try it."

"Go to hell!" Neil pushed her away lightly. "I'm going to tell *Dada* [11] you smoke." He lit another.

Tuli looked at him, "Yah, yah, tattler. *'Dada, Dada*, your wife smokes'," she imitated nastily. Then turned to him, "Why don't you simply say you don't like girls smoking?"

Neil kept quiet.

"That you don't like girls smoking, drinking. You are basically a superstitious, conservative and a coward old man, you know!"

Neil shook his head seriously. "No, not that… you plan to have a baby."

"So? I'm just taking a drag from you. I'm not smoking every day."

She became angry and nodded her head, "Shit! You make me feel like shit!" and threw the cigarette into the water.

Neil laughed. "Sweetheart," he whispered.

Tuli closed her eyes and let her anger melt away. She opened them and looked at Neil. He took a deep drag and tossed almost half of the burning roll into the water.

Tuli smiled at him at this gesture, threw her hands around his neck and kissed him hard on the cheeks.

"Ouch!" said Neil. And turned to her. She cringed her eyes and rolled her lips into a pout and tried to move away from the danger zone. It was too late. Neil cupped her face and kissed her vociferously, sucking her last breath out until she was whining to be set free.

And then that fall!

Neil remembered and smiled. The boat had pulled to the bank and Neil had sprung off to dry land — which was a comfortable couple of feet across. Below that was a dubious zone of mud and silt. Neil turned and offered help to Tuli. She refused. With her sari *anchal* [12] wound around her waist, she too tried to jump. The next second she was flat on her face on the silt!

Neil laughed aloud and threw the emptied clay cup away. The tea-maker turned to him surprised. He ignored that and began walking towards the bus.

Cathy had luckily reached the bus safely. She held the bus handle and looked around. It seemed she was looking for someone. Neil stopped on his tracks. Cathy stepped onto the bus and looked behind her. She saw Neil and got a little flustered as if she was caught doing something wrong. Quickly turning around, she walked into the bus.

Neil frowned. He was perplexed. Considering the pride they held in controlling their emotions, this Westerner was a little too blatant. He knew she was looking for him. He suddenly knew those initial symptoms. *He also knew there would be no Tuli in his life.*

He got onto the bus. Cathy had peeled a banana and had just taken her first bite. He sat down beside her.

"Why do you people have a weird idea that bananas are not contaminated?"

"Huh?" Cathy had her mouthful. She stopped chewing.

"Do you know how they are grown?"

"Uhu…" Cathy shook her head, her eyes genuinely doubtful about the so-dependable edible stuff that was half-way inside her.

"See, Indian soil is not right for the growth of bananas. Particularly hilly soils. So what happens…" Neil controlled a bursting urge to smile as he conjured up this horror-tale, "Fresh manure has to be used."

Cathy gulped down the food. She had little choice. "Fresh manure?"

"Yes. Humans' is best."

"What…?" She opened her mouth. She looked at her banana as though she was looking at an insect. Then tightened her lips at a decision. "Did somebody tell you, you are horrible?"

"Yes," Neil smiled.

"Who?" She was perplexed.

"You. Just now."

She got flustered. "Ca… can you just spare me a minute and let me finish my food?"

Neil shrugged. "I was only trying to help."

"Oh!" She turned away. "You've been such a wonderful one. I wish I could make you disappear."

Neil smiled and looked away. "You know, I like you."

"I don't," Cathy smiled cheekily and attacked her banana.

CHAPTER 6

Manikaran, October 9 1996

Manikaran is the short stopover before the actual trek to Pulga. The small hill station was dotted with *dharmashalas* [13], *gurdwars* [14], small hotels, travel agents' offices and a number of shops lined up selling ethnic goods.

Cathy had fallen asleep on the window pane and Neil watched her, wanting to turn her into Tuli. Other than that, the rest of the hour journey was not too remarkable. The bus stopped at the mouth of a suspension bridge, which was swaying lightly in the breeze, crossing over the whirling Parvati River. Neil strapped his bag on his back and pulled down Cathy's rucksack from the shelf. Even before she could protest he had walked away with it to alight from the bus.

He looked around, trying to figure out which way led to the nearest hotel. Then suddenly heard a clamor. He looked behind and saw a group of six to seven men trying to mob Cathy, each trying to convince her in their broken English permuted with Hindi, to avail their hotels. Cathy stood in their middle, stunned, unable to move.

Neil rushed to her. He held her hand and snapped at the men around, *"Yeh meri biwi hain! Kya baat hain?"*

The words worked like magic. The mob instantly thinned. Only two stood and tried their last attempts in convincing Neil how good their hotel was.

Neil snapped in the same tone, *"Ek baat karo!* One of you speak. What do you want?"

Cathy tried to release her hand. Neil held it only tighter.

"Sir, we have a double-bed room facing the mountains," said the bulkier of the two. The other man, lean and tall, took no time to realize he had lost a foreign customer, which meant a grand fleece. Mumbling something inane under his breath, he walked off.

Neil held Cathy's hand and started walking. The other man straggled along with them. "Sir, Hotel Mount View…sir, excellent food, attached bath sir…"

Neil walked along. *"Mein doondh loonga. Ab aap jayiye.* (I'll find one, you may go.)"

He pulled at Cathy's arm and stepped onto the bridge. The man finally gave up. He too mumbled something incongruous and walked off.

No sooner they were alone, Cathy jerked her hand free. "What did you tell them?"

"I told them you were my wife." Neil was serious.

Cathy flushed; "Of all nerves…" she snatched her bag from Neil's shoulders.

"Hey, look miss, you have been travelling in India for some time. You know all this. You should have been able to handle them."

"I had just been to Delhi. I have never faced this thing before," she said honestly with her hand waving in the air.

She paused a while. "What did they want anyway? Me?"

Neil looked at her, "You think you are that irresistible? They wanted green bucks, dollars."

"But I don't possess any. I have a few Swiss Francs and Indian rupees."

"They didn't know that. You didn't exactly advertise it."

Cathy was exasperated. Then she suddenly remembered. "And what were they saying about a double-bed room?"

Neil looked staid. "Yah! We have to sleep in the same room."

Cathy burst out. "You're **mad!** You think you can get away with all this?" She started walking faster. "Why don't you simply *go?*"

"Okay, calm down," Neil was serious. "We'll sleep with our backs towards each other."

Cathy threw her bag at him.

They crossed the bridge on foot. The crystal clear water of this tributary of Yamuna River danced joy-rides over colored boulders. The bridge swayed. Sprays of cool water swung into their faces. Cathy crossed her arms and held herself. It was chilly.

Across the bridge, there was a crowd of shops exhibiting various ethnic — precious stones, Indian jewelry and wood carvings, before the hilly road crept up to a few hotels daubed over the hill. Cathy looked at the contents of a shop and moved into it.

A boy, about two-and-a-half years of age, dawdled up to Neil's knees and extended a small hand up. *"Paisa..."* [15]

Neil looked down. He had no shoes, a tattered sweater and grim pants. His dusty overgrown hair fell over his eyes. His nose was running and he was not bothered about it. His other hand was pulling up the pant falling off from his thin waist.

My son would have been this high... I would never have left him out in the cold like this....

He jerked the thought away and handed the boy a coin.

He walked towards Cathy. She was busy trying to purchase a bead necklace. Neil went and stood beside her. She glanced at him. "You're not gone?" she jested. He looked away grimly towards the river.

"What's the matter, you're not yourself?" Cathy asked seriously.

"No I'm fine," He smiled. "Is that for you?"

Cathy slowly lowered her eyes. And then looked at the beads. "Yes." She quickly bought the necklace and said, "Come on, let's go."

While walking Cathy came close to him and held his arm. "You know, in the entire trip, this is the first time I'm seeing a different look on your face." She looked at him.

Neil looked at her and suddenly found her unbearable.

"Neil," This was the first time she pronounced his name. It sounded weird. "I don't know you at all. But you filled up my journey with so much fun that I do not want to forget you."

She took out the beaded necklace and held it out for him. "This is for you or your girlfriend. Please. I want to give it to you."

Neil stopped on his tracks. "But you bought it for yourself?"

"I'll buy another. Or you buy one for me. But I want you to take this."

Neil took it and smiled, letting out a short breath. His eyes unabashedly scanned the crowd of children playing near the bridge. He didn't see the boy.

Cathy followed his eyes and turned. He immediately put on his guards and said, "Come, you chose one for yourself."

They walked across to another curio shop and Cathy chose an ornate wooden photo-stand. Neil paid for it. They were silent as they walked towards a hotel.

The hotel was a pink colored two-storey building with a white, vertical signboard hanging across the floors that said *Hotel Manikaran* and below it, horizontally, *Exceptional fooding and lodging*.

Neil walked towards the reception and said, "Two single rooms, with attached baths."

The man quickly looked at Cathy and asked, "Would you like rooms facing the mountain?"

"Sure."

"They would be a little costlier."

"That's okay."

They were lucky. Their rooms were also adjacent. Apparently this wasn't the rush season and the hotel was practically empty.

A bell-boy led them up the stairs. The rooms weren't exquisite, but neat. Neil's room had a single bed with a neat white bedspread. A side table, a cabinet and a bathroom.

He stubbed his cigarette into a wooden ashtray on the side-table and placed his rucksack on the floor. He paid the bellboy five rupees and took the room's lock and key.

Then coming out, he locked his door. He went over to Cathy's room. A long balcony ran across, with four rooms including theirs', facing the river and the snow-peaked mountains. It was October and the air was exceptionally chilly.

Cathy's door was ajar. She had unzipped her rucksack and was taking out her garments. He knocked on the door.

Cathy turned, "Oh!" she said, "Hi!"

"Let's eat. I'm famished."

"Yeah. Just hold on. I'll settle myself."

"Go ahead. I'll wait outside."

"No, no. You can come in."

Neil smiled and walked in. He looked around. Her room was no different from his. Cathy had placed a few cosmetics on her side table. She took out her soap-case, paste and brush and went inside the bathroom.

"Will they provide us with hot water?" She came out and asked.

"I don't know. We'll find out."

"It's incredibly cold. I think I'll ask for another blanket."

Neil suddenly threw himself on the bed and lay on his back, supporting his head with his hands folded beneath it and said.

"You don't need any. You can have me."

Cathy looked at him shocked. Then she came charging down and hit him hard on the stomach. "You're back to your old self, aren't you?" and blushed.

Neil laughed aloud. "You know you blush like a typical Indian girl."

She turned away and zipped up her rucksack. She snatched her purse from underneath him and held out her hand.

"Let's go."

Neil looked at her deeply and then took her hand. Cathy pulled him up.

They walked downstairs to the dining hall and sat down. The dining hall was dim and cozy with the windows closed and a fire in the fireplace, flickering at a corner. The wooden framework ran across the walls above the heavy curtains and the dark wooden furniture set a dangerously passionate arena.

Cathy sat opposite him and placed a purse on the table, "I'll pay."

Neil raised his eyebrows and looked at her, not giving any importance to the words.

She was wearing a navy blue jacket over her mauve pullover. A small gold chain dangled from her neck on top of the pullover. Her white fingers placed on the table had three golden rings. Her near-white tresses hung around her face as she scrutinized the menu card. Her eyebrows were black.

"I'll have and egg and jam-toast," she said, looked up and found Neil looking at her. "Hello?" she held out the card, "What about you?"

"Huh…" Neil said but did not remove his eyes from her face. "You've got very striking eyes."

She looked away. Then turned and said, "Look whatever you have in mind, keep it within you, okay. I am in no mood to have an affair with you."

Neil smiled and leant back on the chair. "You are going to miss out a lot."

The waiter came to their table at that instant and said, "Yes sir?"

Neil sat up. He turned the menu card around and said, "Jam-toast and omelet for the lady. And ummm… four *puris* [16] and *alu-bhaji* [17] for me." He looked at Cathy, "Coffee? Black or white?"

"Black." She turned away in disgust.

"Milk for me. Make it snappy."

"Yes sir." The waiter took the menu card and walked away. Another couple sat at the other end of the room. They seemed to be newly married with the girl wearing thick red *sindoor* smeared on her hair parting and an incongruous matching of a sweater and trousers, with the conventional red and white bangles on her wrists — the kind Bengali women wear right after getting married. Her dark, ominous-looking husband was engrossed in her and she seemed a little embarrassed.

Tuli would never wear those. She was crazy…

"You Indian men are like beggars…" Neil got startled at the words. He looked at her and tried to concentrate. His mind had been way off. "…You pounce on white women as if you've never seen women all your life. As if white women are always available!" She was furious.

Neil leant forward. "I beg your pardon? Look lady," He tried to understand her. "Look Cathy. I didn't mean to hurt you. I understand that your travel in India wasn't a pleasant one. What you said about Indian men is very true…."

"Yeah." Cathy cut in, liking his words. "Yeah, they're like… they're like --- vultures…" She recoiled in hatred. "See at the look in their eyes. I don't know why people come to India. It has such horrible people."

She shook her head and held her forehead. "I'm sorry. I shouldn't have spoken like this." She removed her hand and looked at him. "You, you made me speak like this," she said waving a finger at him. "Look," she tried to calm herself. "I like you. I've enjoyed your company a lot. But I don't like the look in your eyes."

Neil reached out and held her hand. "It's okay. I'm sorry. I don't have any such intentions. I was just pulling your leg. Okay?"

Cathy leant back and looked at him dubiously, "You're sure?"

"Absolutely."

She closed her eyes. "It's all right. I'm okay."

Neil continued holding her hand. Looking deeply into her eyes he said, "I haven't put the idea off either."

Before Cathy could react, he pounced on the other hand and said, "I'll tell you something." He smiled. "This time an honest confession. I've had no dearth of women all my life. I am 23 and have slept with over… ummm… 20 women in the past two years."

Cathy was disgusted and tried to release her hand. Neil held it tighter.

"You want me to leave your hand?"

"Yes. If you don't mind."

He let go of her hands and leant back. "See, if you really think I am unsafe to be with… well… fine… we won't bother each other again." He became serious and took out a cigarette from his pocket.

She looked at him. And broke into a smile. An inviting smile. A very warm, friendly smile.

Neil waved the cigarette at her, "Now what is that supposed to mean?"

Cathy looked up at the ceiling, smiling. "Why did I ever meet you?"

The food arrived. Neil kept his cigarette aside and attacked the delights.

"You know something?" Cathy spoke after gorging down the first few bites. "You are a wonderful person."

Neil shook his head. "You don't know a thing."

She looked at him surprised, "What do you mean?"

Neil took a hearty bite into the rolled *puri* and chewed on it comfortably making her wait. After gulping it down, he looked at her.

"I am not a good person."

"Well, I didn't find you so bad. What's it that's bad about you?"

"You'll be scared." He attacked his last *puri*.

"Why should I be scared?"

Neil slowly finished his last bites. Then leant back.

"I am a criminal. I was involved in a murder."

Her mouth fell open. She had a piece of omelet in it. She quickly chewed in down and shook her head. "You're joking." She stated confidently.

Neil shook his head too. "I told you you'd be scared."

She kept shaking her head. "Er… *pardon me?* You mean… you mean… you are a fugitive? You mean… I mean… *Why?*" She ended with the big question.

Neil laughed, "Why?" A good question. "Why?" He turned serious. "I got paid for it," he shrugged.

Cathy forgot her breakfast. She ran her nervous fingers through her hair. "Er…" She opened her mouth to say something but was too stunned to speak. She looked around. "Somebody please save me from this person!" She turned to him. "You know I can call the police?"

Neil laughed, "You can't prove a thing. I had a good lawyer. I am a free man now."

"Neil, you know, this is not…" she waved around her hands nervously, "this is not done. I enjoyed the breakfast with you but let's part ways. I cannot get involved with a criminal."

"That's okay with me, if you really think that way. You were so inquisitive about me so I thought of letting you know my past."

"That's all right. But this is ridiculous. You're a criminal. What are you doing? Running away from the police?"

"No… You didn't hear me? The case was over a month ago. Now I am a free man. They couldn't prove me guilty. In fact," He shrugged, "I got involved with this gang war in Mumbai just by chance. I had gone there to stay with a friend who was into these things. I simply helped him throw a man off a forty-four-storeyed building."

"WHAT…???!!!!" Cathy gasped. "And where is your friend?"

"He's serving his term."

"Jesus Christ!" She gasped again and held her head.

"Cathy, you are stuck with a very dangerous man. But don't worry. I won't harm you. In fact, I am falling in love with you."

"Stop it!" She almost screamed. The couple at the other end turned to look at her. Cathy raised her hand. "I don't want to have anything to do with you."

"Okay, let's part ways," Neil got up. "Shall we?"

Cathy stood up. She forgot the coffee. Neil walked up to the reception and said, "Cancel the coffees."

He leapt up the stairs and headed for his room. Cathy followed with slow strides. Neil was inside his room trying to scold himself for trusting Cathy so much. He only knew her for a few hours. How could he trust her so much? He looked at his watch. Eleven thirty. He had to stay here for the rest of the day and night and then begin the trek at dawn. He felt claustrophobic. He thought of walking out for some fresh air.

There was a knock on the door. He turned. Cathy was standing. She walked in.

"I want to talk to you."

"Come in," he said off-handed. "Please, sit down."

She sat down on the bed. "Why don't you sit too?" She pointed at the bed.

He sat down.

Cathy said, "I'm sorry for being so harsh. But… why did you get into all this mess? You're sure you are a free man?"

He nodded. He was still frowning. He still didn't trust her.

She sensed that. "You see, I'll leave India in a few days. Your secret will go with me. So you can trust me."

He looked down.

She said, "Don't misunderstand me. Anyone would have reacted like that to such a revelation." She reached out and held his hand. She held it with both her hands and looked deep into his eyes. "I like you very much."

Neil stopped frowning. He sighed. The same wicked smile lit up his face. He slowly pulled her towards him. Magnetized, she moved near him. He held her face up to his. Cathy closed her eyes. Neil waited. Letting the hunger grow. She opened her eyes questioningly. He smiled, "May I?"

She smiled back. "You may not," she whispered.

"Okay." Neil played with her tresses.

"Stop it!" Cathy pulled his lips onto hers and their parted lips met hungrily, adroitly, arousing fire through each follicle and cell membrane. Neil suddenly jerked up, walked up to the door and bolted it.

Then there was no looking back. He hungrily leapt onto her and threw her on the bed. Within minutes their naked bodies met like fireworks. Time was a complete washout. They forgot their lunch. They forgot the cold and the blankets. As two primitive warriors, they tore at each other to explore and satiate their hunger that had been, all this time, rising like a volcanic eruption...

TULI

CHAPTER 1

Calcutta and Katoa, February 1994 to September 1994

Tuli was born on the day of the solar eclipse. A full solar eclipse, with a diamond ring. However, she was not to be born on that day. Her mother's delivery date was ten days away. Srimati, the plump woman in her late twenties was expecting her second child. Her first one was a boy of five. She desperately hoped for a daughter this time. She sat surrounded by the women of the house, her two sisters-in-law.

The tales tell that if you cut fish or vegetables on the day of solar eclipse while you are pregnant, you'd have a child with fingers and toes chopped off. If you saw the eclipse, lunar or solar, you'd have a blind child.

But nobody in this house believed in it, least of all Srimati herself. She crept upstairs with her giggly sisters-in-law to view the eclipse and got scolded by her husband, Gopal Nagchowdhury, for it.

Gopal ran a business of packaging along with his brother and his widowed sister, as partners. Their parents had died early in a car accident and they grew up under the loving wings of their father's only brother and only sister who were both unwed. Their uncle was now dead and aunt was aged, but still commanded the same respect in household decisions.

There was a reason for that.

Damayanti, the crux and the driving force of the entire unit, was in her late fifties, active and fun loving and was referred to by everyone as *Chhotoma*, which meant 'youngest mother'. When her elder brother and sister-in-law died in a car accident thirty years back, she was hopelessly in love with her music tutor and all plans were being made for their marriage. The ceremony got postponed for a year due to the tragedy.

By the end of the year, when her widow mother and her prospective groom once again tried to reschedule the marriage, she refused. And took charge of the three little orphans, the youngest girl being only one-and-a-half-years old.

Her brother got busy trying to make a living through a business, constructed the house, gave the three children the education and upbringing they needed and forgot all about getting married.

Damayanti was barely educated, but read books from all over the world, could dance the Waltz and cook *biryani*, a Mughal delicacy. She ran the household on one note — discrepancy. Each of her nephew and niece were encouraged to different sets of ideas about life. At the same time, along with their distinctive existences, there was a fine thread of harmony attached, by which they all respected each other's viewpoint. There was a distinct chaos in the family, the foremost created by *Chhotoma* herself, yet each one was free to perform at will — which resulted in the best harmonious situation of all.

They had impromptu drenching sessions in the first rains at their courtyard, which was led by Damayanti herself. She suddenly threw parties in the middle of the night at the terrace, waking up the kids, her brother and her mother and sang *Rabindrasangeet* [118] under the moonlight. The kids yawned and slowly crept downstairs back to sleep. She never stopped anyone, but gave everyone the taste of living life like a non-conformist.

Even when she got her two nephews married within a short time of each other, from girls of varied backgrounds, she continued her probationary eccentricity with them. She suddenly emerged from the kitchen at noon, one day, after a comfortable period of disappearance, yawning, saying, "Let's not eat today. I don't feel like cooking."

The two newly-weds looked at each other and rushed into the kitchen. By afternoon they were ready with *khichri* [19] sweating and angry at their husband's aunt. However, their object of antagonism was performing one of her vanishing tricks. She was seen nowhere. They knew she had gone to a nearby derelict temple, and was sitting there until she felt better.

She was not a performer, but an essential traveler. She rested whenever she felt out of place in the world.

It was easy to misunderstand her. But it was easier to understand her. She was forever close to being jettisoned as redundant, but for the education she bestowed upon her children who were not born out of her womb. So she remained the nub, the nerve of the whole unit.

She died at 60 — smiling and happy till the end, while the whole house wept, four years before Tuli's birth.

CHAPTER 2

The pain came while Srimati was rushing down the stairs. She was at once made to lie down. The pain came in small spurts. Like a wave. Filling her up until she moaned and then letting her go. Gopal came rushing back from work and took her to the hospital.

Tuli was born very quickly, bang in the middle of the eclipse. It was an esoteric darkness outside and the crows cawed confused, wondering why the day had ended so quickly. The entire town of Katoa was out in the streets trying to view this marvel. A nurse came out smiling with the baby girl wrapped in white and nibbling her fingers. Everyone was happy.

It was the second brother's idea to call Mahibabu.

Partho was an introvert and slightly superstitious. And wondered if the eclipse would have an effect on the child.

After a while, he sighed and nodded with a slight click of his tongue. "Okay... okay future". He realized he wasn't convincing and decided to come straight to the point. He looked up and said, "Keep her carefully. She will bring darkness to her life. Get her married to a good family as soon as you can. She has a short life. Getting her *gotrantar* would help." *Gotrantar* meant getting her married to a family with a different *gotra* [20].

Srimati started weeping and the men kept their calm. They decided not to emotionally involve themselves too much with the child. They were scared of their own pains.

The fair baby had other ideas. With large black eyes and a captivating smile she did something that Mahibabu forgot to predict

— she stole their hearts. A toothless smile at the age of six months, when she was given her first plate of rice, accompanied by a ceremony, melted all walls of indifference that her father, uncle and aunt thought they would hold for her. They all fell in love with her. Thus began her passionate affair with the world she was to live in for a few days.

As she grew up, one comparison became apparent.

It happened one day when the first thunderstorm struck Bengal, after periods of ceaseless humidity. The windows and doors banged repeatedly. Srimati and Mahima, the other brother's wife, were running helter-skelter trying to block out the reeling madness.

Mahima first saw her.

Six-year-old Tuli was standing at the edge of the terrace which had no boundary. Her shoulder-length hair was flying wildly and her hands were thrown up towards the sky, as the big drops fell.

Mahima screamed! She was not seeing Tuli! *She was seeing Damayanti!*

That day it began. The comparison. And they became slowly convinced that Damayanti could not leave them. She had to be reborn.

As Tuli!

CHAPTER 3

Little Tuli was oblivious to the anxiousness going around about her. She wondered why she was always reprimanded for anything she did, while her brother and her younger cousin comfortably got away with it. She learnt lot later she was to die early and half-believed the filtered-in story. She felt funny and wondered what it felt like to die.

Tuli excelled in her education. But she wasn't interested in it. It was right after Srimati's husband died when Tuli was 16, that she realized the responsibility of her daughter and decided to get Tuli married. Tuli's education was stopped as soon as she finished her schooling. She somehow missed it.

The Roys in Calcutta were Gopal*babu*'s clients. Soumen, the eldest son of the family was chosen for 18-year-old Tuli. He was a graduate and a cost accountant and was in the family business. A swelling proposition and they had liked the fair little Tuli.

The prospective groom was twenty-five and light-featured. He had curly black hair, was sans moustache and wore 'rimless' glasses. He looked more like a dependable doctor.

He was, however, a man with intense physical desires. Tuli's skin first struck him. If it was so light on the parts that were 'exposed', what could it be like inside? He mentally stripped the girl the first day he saw her. She was sitting opposite him on a sofa, wearing a peacock blue silk sari with white jasmine flowers on her hair. Her body was concealed from her chest to her ankle but Soumen noticed the accentuated fairness going down from her neck into her chest. The silk sari was pleated on her breasts and Soumen visualized them to be small and warm. He felt his breath coming in spurts and tightness beneath his underpants.

She sensed his gaze and looked up with her wide eyes to meet his, examining her breasts. He got flustered. He couldn't wait to get married!

It took a month for the arrangements. Tuli was married on the eleventh day of March.

Two days of rituals preceded the actual marriage. She was pulled out of bed at wee hours of the winter dawn and made to undergo several weird rituals. She had to cut the water of their pond with a piece of metal, before sunrise, which she felt very silly about and eat puffed rice with curd. Then several strings were tied on her left hand and below her waist, which, her relatives informed her cheekily, would be untied by her husband on the night of *phulsojya* [21].

Her friends came and informed her that they had got their admission in colleges. She looked out of her window to the sky and wanted to fly away.

She was constantly pulled beside Soumen and pushed in front of him for various marriage details, in Katoa and in Calcutta. Once he had his arms around her for a ritual as they dropped puffed rice on fire from a plate. She stiffened when she felt his hardness stuck sharply behind her.

After the ceremony in Katoa, she went to Calcutta in a trance and forgot to cry when she left her family. Instead she consoled everybody around her who wept inconsolably. In Calcutta she went through two days in a trance. A very busy boy, a little older than her, came often and asked her in her ears, "Are you hungry?" "Are you thirsty?" "Are your legs paining?" She replied every time with a "No" and wondered who he was. Later she learnt he was Neil, her brother-in-law.

At her reception she was bedecked like an Indian goddess with a floral crown and a floral garland and was asked to sit and smile. Her eyes stung with tears when she saw her mother for the first time after two days and realized she wasn't a part of her any more. She was about to burst into tears when she saw the cameramen swarming in to witness and click the scene. She gulped down her tears and smiled for the first time in three days.

All were disappointed.

CHAPTER 4

Neil watched the scene from a distance and felt a burning abhorrence for the hypocrisies of the rituals. The poor girl, he thought, and now she would have to go through the legalized prostitution called *phulsojya*. He had already seen his brother giggling and happy with his friends as the hour arrived. His friends presented him with a carton of condoms and told him how lucky he was to be able to finger such a wonderful skin.

"All women are the same," he overheard Raja saying, "but a fair one is the best."

"Go slow man, she's quite a kid," said Niloy.

"Come on, man. See what happens when you wait?" said Aneek. "Somu never visited those ugly alley cats we did. So now he's got a beauty under him. Literally!"

They all laughed. Soumen felt proud of possessing a figure that everyone envied so much. He couldn't wait till they all left.

By midnight, guests had all left and Tuli was ushered into a bedecked room with a flowery mosquito net over a huge bed, which she was told was her bedroom. Her mother had furnished the room with new furniture, which she felt an immediate attachment to.

The photographer and Soumen's friends crowded into the room as they insisted that they take a few 'romantic' photographs. Soumen held Tuli's hand and pulled her to the bed. She wriggled to free her hand, but Soumen held it only tighter. She gave up. He put his hands around her as the photographer clicked.

"Closer," his friends cried.

Soumen made her get up and pulled her onto his lap. She felt she sat on something hard as he clutched her around her stomach. The friends were smiling and felt hard inside their pants. They would all have to go to the bathroom after this photo session. They wanted more.

Soumen lay down and made her lie down beside her. He placed his hands over her stomach. He felt very smart and suave. Tuli's every muscle went stiff.

"A kiss, come on…" cried the spectators. Soumen looked at her. Her lips were small and red. He held her face and turned it.

Tuli didn't know when she slapped him… when she freed her hand and hit him hard across his temple!

He instantly sat up. His smile vanished as he held his temple. She felt scared seeing the look in his eyes. He looked like a hyena whose food had been snatched away. He let her go. Only for a while. As if to wait for the next weak moment when he'd pounce on her again.

The crowd felt their organs go limp.

The photographer stood up. "We'll leave. Let's leave." They all left one by one. "See you later," they told a stunned Soumen. Tuli felt guilty and sat up.

She went across and bolted the door. She found Soumen sitting in the same position and looked as if he didn't know how to react.

She smiled. "You're tired." It was half a question. He was her husband and she remembered that she was supposed to be nice to him. "Let's sleep."

She went to the dressing table and took off her jewelry one by one. He was angry, insulted. But her reflection in the mirror and that skin made him gulp. He wanted to forgive her.

He got down from the bed and walked over to her. Standing beside her, he eyed her from head to toe. He stripped her mentally and felt his male hardness thump.

"Tuli," he added the warmest spice in his voice. "Do you know how beautiful you are?"

"Yes," she took off her veil.

He was at a loss for words. "You know?"

"Yes, everybody tells me." She took off her bangles. "But I know… my nose is blunt."

She walked away to open her suitcase for a change of clothes.

Soumen followed her, magnetized. "You know what tonight signifies?"

She turned, wide-eyed. "Yes. Tonight is *phulsojya*."

"And what does *phulsojya* mean?"

"It means we go to bed for the first time." She took out her nightdress and undergarments and walked into the bathroom.

He was once again at a loss for words. He floundered to handle the situation correctly. He sat limp on a stool and tried to grope for a method that would arouse her. He never realized it would be so difficult. He wanted to consult his friends and was angry with them for not telling him about a situation like this. He decided he'd simply pounce on her and rape her. She wouldn't scream and nobody in this house would mind anyway, even if she did. But his temple still stung as he remembered the slap. And he didn't have the courage. And he didn't think it was right.

In that order.

She came out and gave him a smile. She was wearing an orange night-suit, which left her arms and neckline a little too bare. He thrust his hands into his thighs and clutched onto his hardness. It was impossible! He felt he could never take her to bed.

His friends were wrong. He did have a few sessions with those ugly black women lined up at crossroads. They were so giving. He had practiced the art well. He wondered where he had gone wrong.

Tuli lay down on the bed and pulled her blanket over herself. It was chilly and she clutched the blanket up to her chin, crouching underneath it.

She then tilted her head on the pillow and said, "Let's be friends first, then we can have our *phulsojya*, okay? Today, I am squashed." She turned over, "Goodnight," she said. In a few minutes she was breathing heavily and fast asleep.

CHAPTER 5

Soumen woke up the next day around mid-morning. He remembered he was on leave. That he had got married. Suddenly he remembered Tuli and a bitter taste filled his mouth. He turned to see her.

Her side of the bed was neatly done. Her suitcase was locked .The bathroom door was ajar and smelt wet and fresh. The bedroom door was unbolted.

He sat up. She must have woken up very early. He looked at their new clock hung over their new dressing table. It was past eight-thirty. Not so late. He could do with a bit more sleep. But he wanted to find Tuli. After all, he was her husband. She could get lost in this big house.

CHAPTER 6

Neil had a nightmare. He dreamt of a man slicing off a naked girl's throat with a chopper. The girl wriggled and kicked her legs as he sliced her stomach. Then there were quite a few of them. One of them was his brother and one was him. He woke up with a start. He was breathing heavily and shivering. He was aghast at the nightmare!

He had gone to sleep pretty late after a number of chores his mother assigned him to. Being the younger of the two, and the most eligible person to do all the legwork, he was the obvious errand boy for the elders. Neil never felt fatigued. He liked his new sister-in-law, his 'boudi' [25]. Somehow that propelled him. He could have quietly slipped off to smoke a 'joint' in his college because he knew everyone was capable of doing just everything without him. But he stuck on. Her uncomplaining, indefatigable attitude somehow intrigued him. He stayed on so that he didn't miss out on anything.

He walked out of his room onto the huge adjoining terrace and stretched a little. The terrace was in tiers; each tier three or four steps higher or lower than the other. There were several exits to go downstairs; every exit within a walled enclosure. So all in all, the expanse looked like an excellent spot for a little hide-and-seek. It looked wonderful in daylight. Strings ran across bamboo poles where the clothes were hung, and high, thick and ornate cement railings adorned the boundary. But at night, there were stories of ghosts. With just two light-watt bulbs burning, the terrace looked something out of a haunted house.

Neil had his room improvised with his computer, a bed, a cupboard and a study table. He had laid white floor tiles and lovely pastel-green wallpaper. It was an old haunted room that he transformed into a magical corner for himself. He did that against all odds.

His mother let him have his room on condition that he would sleep downstairs with his brother. He had agreed immediately and had broken his promise later on.

The sun was up. Most of the womenfolk would be as well, he assumed. Suddenly he saw a little flutter of blue on his right, on the next tier. He moved towards it and saw his *boudi* standing in a blue sari, against the railing, facing the sunrise. Her hair was wet and loose, and most of her jewelry taken off. The golden rays made her face appear amber.

He hesitated a moment. Then he walked down the steps towards her. She jumped when she saw him.

"Hi!" She smiled despite the scare.

"You're up?" Neil asked.

"Yes, I wake up early."

Then she looked at his attire in a vest and a *pajama* and assumed, "You slept over here?"

"Yeah, that's my kingdom."

"Yah? Such a nice place to stay." She obviously wanted to go in. Neil wasn't sure whether he could invite her in. What would his brother, whom he called '*Dada*', think?

"Come in. Have a look."

He led her up the stairs and into his room. He quickly glanced around before stepping in so as not to leave behind any witnesses and undue tension because of this.

Tuli walked in unhesitant. "Wow! You have a computer!" she beamed.

"Yes." He suddenly wished he could say he had bought it with his own money. But could not. His dad had bought it for him. Neil had told him that it was a loan and that he'd pay back.

She sat down on the chair and said, "Will you teach me how to use a computer?"

Neil shrugged. "Okay. We'll have plenty of time."

She seemed to like the idea. Suddenly she looked out of the window and was lost in her own thoughts.

Neil sat down on another chair and picked up his cigarettes.

"You don't mind if I smoke?"

"No, no, even I smoke." She replied smiling and turned on her attention to the stabilizer under the table, oblivious to the effect she had on him.

Before he could react, she had switched on the stabilizer with her toe.

"It works this way, right?"

"Yes." He forgot to light his smoke as he hurried towards her.

She looked up and smiled. "Don't worry, I know how to start one," and switched on the power button.

A sexy picture of Pamela Anderson appeared on the screen in a moment.

He was embarrassed and hated himself for being so callous. His *boudi*, however, remained unperturbed and examined the voluptuous body as she waited for the hourglass to disappear.

Then she lost interest and sighed. "I must go, Soumen will be up."

Neil shrugged. He wanted to find out what put her off.

"I'm… er… sorry about the picture…"

"What picture?" She looked surprised. And then looked at the screen. "Oh! Pamela Anderson? No, no, it's all right. She's got a beautiful figure."

She was obviously more knowledgeable than he thought her to be. And so much different… *Dada* was very lucky, he added in his thoughts.

CHAPTER 7

Their house had thirteen members and four servants. Neil's mother, Mahamaya, was the nucleus of the joint family. She presided over both the kitchen and the prayer room; instructed the cook, Manik, what to prepare, when and for whom.

The nub of the house was the sprawling dining hall adjoining a vast kitchen, where specific timings were maintained for individual food habits and where the family was to assemble everyday at dinner. Mahamaya was an exceptionally organized person and her rules and routines rarely missed the clock.

Unmistakably, she was the busiest person in the house. She ruled over her kingdom like a queen. Ever since her mother-in-law died of cancer four years ago, she had been very conscious, logical, analytical, yet understanding of her family's needs. At the same time, she never wavered from her path of truth and made every effort to bind the family together.

It had been no easy task, considering that the other two wives, who were teachers, tried in every way to untie the bond. She had to deal with various mood swings, including that of her husband's and her younger son's, and furiously gossiping sisters-in-law who often ganged up against her.

Her elder son was a weakling at heart, but was obedient. He was afraid of committing a blasphemy and hence easier to tackle. Neilu was the quiet and determined one. Rash and too impulsive. He was a budding non-conformist and unpretentiously eluded the rules of the house. His mother was scared for him.

Her younger son inherited this trait from her husband, Digambar Roy, who was forever ready to settle his brothers' dues and disintegrate the business, since they wanted it. He never believed in chaining down anybody for his personal needs. It was Mahamaya who intervened every time such an inauspicious occasion arose and, with her diplomacy and intelligence, disposed of the notions. She was such an imposing factor in their lives, that they felt almost incomplete without her.

Except Neil.

Mahamaya woke up before anybody else. Had her bath and worshipped. Till then she never saw anyone's face, barring her husband's and never spoke to anybody. Then she woke up her prime servant, Manik, who was the only servant allowed inside the kitchen.

Manik yawned and went downstairs to pull out a cork from the mouth of a pipe, wherefrom the municipality water rushed out and filled up a near-empty tank called, *chowbachcha* [22], located in a corner of the courtyard. Manik washed his mouth and hands very carefully. 'Ma' was particular about that.

He went upstairs and prepared three cups of tea on the kerosene stove. One for Ma, one for Neil and one for himself. He served tea to Ma who sat on a chair in the balcony and watched the world wake up. Then he took Neil's tea and a charcoal oven up to the terrace. He gave Neil, whom he called *Chhorda*, the tea, and lit the clay oven with charcoal and dried cow dung. That took some time. By then *Chhorda* finished his tea, and he brought the cup downstairs.

Chhorda was a friend and often gave him a drag from his cigarette. But *Dadababu*, Soumen, was different. He was nice to him in front of everyone and even gave him small tips. But alone he was scary. He abused him and treated him like an animal for small mistakes. Manik knew he was in bad company. He had mentioned it to Ma one day. Mahamaya simply nodded and asked him to continue with his work.

Mahamaya knew about his son's whereabouts and the immediate solution that she thought of was getting him married. Gopal Nagchowdhury was a business colleague of her husband. He died rather early. She liked his daughter and had sent the proposal. It got immediately accepted.

CHAPTER 8

Soumen worried about Tuli and thought she must have gone to the prayer room considering the middle-class background she was from. He found his mother coming out of her bedroom.

"Somu? You're up? Want some tea?"

"Hmm…" Soumen nodded.

Mahamaya held her mynah's nest hanging from the ornate arches of the balcony, opened the cage door with one hand and took out its food bowl with the other, to replenish it, while the black bird fluttered.

"Where's Tuli?" she asked. "Still sleeping?"

Soumen shook his head, confused, "I don't know. I didn't see her after I woke up."

She looked perplexed. Manik came down the stairs from the terrace at that moment, with the burning clay oven, and hurried towards the kitchen.

"*Boudi* is in *Chhorda*'s room. They're talking." He let out normally.

But the effect it had was ominous. Both Mahamaya and Soumen fell silent. The former sensed the tension her son felt and smiled, "You go upstairs. I'll send tea for both of you."

He leapt up the stairs to the terrace. Then slowed down his pace. He could see Neilu's room from where he stood on the stairs. The window was open. He couldn't see Neilu. But he saw Tuli sitting in front of the computer, talking and smiling to him.

He felt awkward to face Tuli after last night. And he never shared a good rapport with his brother. And he wanted to retrace his steps. But an ego filled his soul. She belonged to him. He'd better bring her back.

He walked into the room.

"Hi!" said Tuli "Good Morning!"

He nodded "Good Morning." And sat down on the bed and stretched.

A silence followed which Neil tried to mask. "What plans do you both have, are you going on a honeymoon?"

"I've booked for Digha."

"Seaside? But I prefer the mountains." Tuli looked sad.

"We'll go there some other time."

"Why can't we go now?" she asked like an obstinate child.

Soumen got a little irked. "I have already done the bookings."

Tuli fell silent. Neil felt bad for her. *Dada* could have been a little more patient, he felt.

"*Dada*," said Neil trying to change the topic, "*Boudi* wants to learn computers. Why don't you enroll her in a class?"

Soumen smiled, "You teach her. Let her develop the interest, then I'll enroll her."

Tuli suddenly felt claustrophobic. She got up. "I'm going downstairs. I think I'll go and see Ma."

Both the brothers were left in silence as she suddenly walked out. Soumen looked at Neil disgustingly, the intense jealousy he felt within him all this while, came forth once they were alone. Then he followed Tuli downstairs.

CHAPTER 9

Digha, March 15, 1994

The newlyweds started for Digha by a tourist bus the next morning. They had planned to stay for two nights and three days and return by bus, too. They had a hotel booked over there with a private beach and a park, the best one in the small seaside tourist spot — a six-hour drive from Calcutta.

The roads were initially rough and Tuli felt nauseated. She sat by the window and closed her eyes. The wind swept the loose strands of her hair that escaped from her braid wild over her face. She wore a yellow, floral *salwar-kameez* and a red *bindi* on her forehead. She wore a bit of *kajal* [23] in her eyes and a red-tinted lipstick.

She looked something out of a fairytale book and Soumen felt restless at not being able to possess her completely till then.

They had a two-seater to themselves. Soumen took the opportunity when he saw that the other passengers were mostly asleep and kissed her lightly on the cheeks. He decided to be suave and charming. That could win her, he felt.

She immediately opened her eyes. He smiled at her. She smiled back and went back to sleep.

A nice risk taken, he felt. He couldn't wait to get to the hotel.

They got off the bus a little before lunchtime. Tuli saw the ocean for the first time and gasped. Soumen was bringing down the suitcases from the bus when he suddenly saw Tuli missing from his side.

He turned around frantic. And then he saw her. She had walked off onto the beach and was walking towards the sea.

He didn't know how to react. He couldn't call her back. Screaming here would be very conspicuous. He couldn't trust anyone with the luggage. He couldn't carry three suitcases and run after her. He became very angry. He decided to wait for her to turn back.

She didn't. In fact she became quite a tiny spec in the sun as he could make out she had walked into the waters.

What was she up to? Their hotel was a few minutes' walk from where he was. He couldn't risk keeping his luggage over there and then coming back. He feared he would lose her and would have to answer at home about being so irresponsible.

He was just thinking of keeping his luggage in one of the many shops selling stuffs made of shell, that were lining the beach, when he saw her running back. Her feet were sinking in the sand and she panted back with a beaming face.

"I saw a crab! A crab!!" she ran towards him.

He noticed her breasts jumping as she ran and his anger melted.

He smiled, "Tuli, how could you go off like that? I was so worried. You didn't even tell me." He didn't want to sound harsh and make her angry. Knowing by then how moody she was, upsetting her was the last thing on his mind. He had to play very safe.

"Sorry," she continued beaming. "You know those anglers caught so many fish. Let's go and have a bath."

"Yeah sure," he grinned. Of course, why didn't he think of that? "Let's check in first."

"You go. I'll wait for you here."

"No, no, the hotel has a private beach. We'll have a bath there."

"Private beach? You mean it's not the same sea?"

He laughed at her innocence. "No, no. Of course it's the same sea. Only they've enclosed a part of it to own it for their tourists only."

"Own the sea?" She smiled. "You're joking. No one can own the sea."

"No I mean…" he was flustered. He didn't know how to explain. "You wait here. Don't go off anywhere. This place is full of bad people. They'll take off with you." He looked at her. She was so goddamn beautiful! He looked around. The shopkeeper's were having a feast on her. He decided they might just take her off.

He hailed a rickshaw and put the luggage on it. Then he held her hand and said, "Nothing doing, you're coming with me."

"Why?" She stood disobedient, crossing her eyebrows that made a hood over her eyes against the sun.

"Because I cannot stay a minute without you." He felt nice to have said that.

"Of course you can." Tuli was matter-of-fact and wriggled her hand free. She walked into a shop and said, "*Dada*, can I wait here a moment?"

"Of course, *didi* [24]," said a gentle looking middle-aged man. "Please sit down."

Soumen found no choice. He asked the man to take care of her and got onto the rickshaw.

He checked into the hotel fast. It was a nice double-bed room overlooking the sea on the second storey of the hotel. He quickly tipped the bellboy, changed into his shorts and raced for the shop where he left Tuli.

She was not there!

His heart jumped! He charged the man, "Where's my wife?"

The man looked shocked and scared. "I told her not to. But she went towards the sea."

He felt like abusing him. But he didn't want to waste any more time. He ran towards the sea.

Crowds teemed the sea, bathing. He didn't see her. He ran over the sand trying to locate her. He feared she had run away and he'd have to make an explanation back home. Oh! Why couldn't Ma choose a girl with more sanity? This female looked as though she was a bit cracked. How he hated such types. Now if she evolved into someone more insane over the years she would be such an embarrassment!

And then he spotted the bright yellow dress. She was holding an aged-woman by the hand and jumping with the waves. Soumen walked towards her. She was wet and completely oblivious to the dress that clung to her.

"Tuli!" he called her. She turned back and beckoned him with her hand.

He moved towards her magnetized. Her dress was hanging from her breasts, heavy with sand and water and her fair flesh was visible. He felt a familiar throbbing pain inside his shorts. He wanted to possess her sexually. She is his wife, he *should* possess her.

"Hi!" said Tuli when he reached her. "Aunty, this is Soumen, my husband."

He was not interested in the elderly lady and after a quick smile led her away into the water.

"Come with me. Don't be scared."

"But I'm not scared."

They reached waist-deep water and Soumen held her by the waist.

"Now face your back to the waves and jump when it comes."

"How can I jump if I can't see it?" she said after wiping the sand off her face.

"Hold on to me. And jump."

They both jumped. Tuli fell on him and laughed. He too laughed and clung onto her waist. He hadn't gone beyond her waist and decided to do so. He waited for the next wave.

The next one was smaller, and less conducive for his thoughts. She only got a bump from behind and got swept into his arms.

He wound one hand over her neck and one below her breasts. Now this was easier.

He waited. A huge wave followed. And he took the chance. He pulled his hands together to meet, running successfully over her breasts. Oh my God! They were softer and fuller than he imagined! The undergarments had become soft and heavy and posed no obstruction. He continued playing with her assets with no objection from her. And then he ran one hand into her thighs and squeezed her buttocks. He was feeling intoxicated and closed his eyes to bend down to kiss her neck.

She suddenly turned, "You want to make love to me? Then let's go to the hotel."

She jerked herself free and ran over the waters. He followed her in a trance.

They hurried back to the hotel in silence and into their room. And then — Tuli taught him sex.

They were wet and sandy but she never bothered. They had sex on the carpet. She tore off his clothes like a tigress tore at her prey. She took off her own clothes like an expert and pulled down his shorts to look at his biological object that had become overtly conspicuous. She smiled at it and began to play with it like her favorite toy. She completely took charge of him and taught him where her senses laid. She clawed at him like an animal once and became a tame panther another time. Then she wriggled underneath him like a snake and rolled off laughing to make him crawl after her. He died for the climax.

"Not so fast," she whispered.

Then she took him to the bathroom and taught him ecstasy with soap and water. She turned on the shower and knelt in front of him, lifting him into the ionosphere, turning him into a bleating lamb. And then she pulled him on top of her. They lay underneath the soft, warm shower as he reached for the finale. The frantic frenzy drove him into a wildness as Soumen thought, *"Boy, is she experienced!"*

And Tuli thought, *"I think this is how they do it. I think I made him happy."*

What she never realized was right at that moment she was turning the man into her slave whom she could lead on a dance with her little finger. And leading herself into a consequence where he'd be so spellbound with her, lose his sanity whenever she was around and not be able to confront her in the fear of losing out on those wild hours, that she would move towards an unbridled existence where *Soumen would unconsciously become her best guide.*

CHAPTER 10

Calcutta, March 20, 1994

Mahamaya saw a beaming son when they returned and was happy that all was well. He touched her feet and went inside.

After having her bath, Tuli came out fresh and glowing, and a little tanned from the seaside. She was wearing a blouse and her petticoat with her sari wound carelessly around. Soumen went towards her, caught her hand and snatched off her sari. She giggled and tried to free herself. He felt a wild passion clogging his throat, burning his eyes and providing quite an exercise for his male organ. He felt passionately in love with her, her eyes, her smile, her neck, her bosom, her waist, her belly button and everything else. He wanted to die in her arms.

There was a knock on the door. Manik announced lunch. Tuli wrenched herself free. Laughing, she pushed Soumen into the bathroom. "Get a bath, you dirty pig!" She puckered her little nose.

He laughed. He was very happy.

She dressed and came out. In the corridor she met Neil. He had had a bath and was in a blue T-shirt and denim trousers.

"Hi!" beamed Tuli. "You're going out?"

"Yes, I have to get my mark sheet. How was your trip?"

They walked together towards the dining room.

"The sea was great," said Tuli. "I went to bed with him. I didn't like it."

Neil stopped dead on his tracks. He was flustered red. Tuli turned surprised. "What happened?" she asked, shaking the water from her hair.

Neil floundered. "You shouldn't be telling me all this."

"Why? You're a friend," she stated.

Neil resumed his tracks. She was blasphemous! He only hoped she wouldn't shock the other members of the family like this. There would be real trouble then. For a conservative family like them, where rules, norms and social obligations bound the housewives, she would be branded as an anti-social. Was she really immature? Innocent? Or extremely clever? Creating such an effect on purpose? He ruled out the last thought. No. That would be being too sadistic. Maybe she simply didn't know where to say what. Maybe *Dada* should teach her some more social norms. He sensed that her last words had an effect on him, even as he pulled out a chair for her to sit down and sat opposite her. It was such a confident trust she placed in him. He felt like living up to that trust.

He toyed with the salt shaker lost in a completely unprepared-for set of thoughts. Tuli leant over the table and tapped his fingers. "Girlfriend?" she raised her eyebrows.

He smiled and left fiddling with the container. Manik brought the food. Tuli said, "I'll wait for him."

"So would I," Neil added. Manik left.

"Where are the others?" Tuli asked.

"Others? You mean *kakas* (uncles) and *kakis* (aunties)? See, *kakas* are in office and both the *kakis* are in school, teaching. Sujoy and Neepa are in grades eleven and nine. They'll come home at four. Rumpa and Chompa are in grade two and nursery. They are asleep already."

"Who do they stay with? I've never met them properly."

"You haven't met them because you went off right after your marriage day. They were always around. But you know, this household is very disciplined. One has to follow the clock in everything they do and the kids are treated very strictly."

"That must be crazy. Who do they stay with?" she repeated.

"Ma's there. And they have a full-time nanny who feeds them and puts them to sleep."

"Has Ma had her food?" She was an incessant speaker.

"No," Neil smiled. "She'll have her food only after everybody has eaten."

"Why?"

Now Neil turned and asked, "Didn't you have any such strictures in your house?"

"Not really," Tuli pouted her lips. "But there were always special strictures about me."

"Why was that?"

"I don't know," she whined and rested her chin on her hand. "You see, I was born on the day of the solar eclipse and someone predicted that I would die fast and stuff like that."

Neil clicked his tongue at the superstitious minds, which he thought were completely redundant in a lifestyle and nodded.

She continued. "And so my mother was very scared and didn't let me go out much."

"You must have felt terrible."

"Yah, I felt claustrophobic."

"You never rebelled?"

"No, I understood. They were scared that I'll die. But I know that I'll not die now. I want to have a tiny baby with tiny hands and minute toes." She crinkled her eyes for the effect and smiled.

Neil laughed. He visualized the baby and felt nice. Then he remembered something and turned serious. "When did you start smoking?"

"In school."

"In school?" he raised his brows.

"Yah. I used to hide behind the back row and try out each brand during off-periods with the boys of my class."

"And nobody complained?"

"Yes. And I was suspended for a week once," she shrugged.

"So you are a bad girl," Neil leant back.

"No," she stated. "I was good in studies, so I was not a bad girl," she explained categorically.

"Does *Dada* know that you smoke?"

Tuli shook her head. "I didn't feel like smoking in Digha."

"No, but did you tell him?"

"He never asked. And there was no context…"

"No husband ever asked his wife if she smoked, in our household."
He was suddenly possessive about his household. He felt a loyalty
towards his brother and his family, which stemmed from his head
and not from his heart.

"I'm sorry, I should have mentioned…"

"*Boudi*…" Neil leant forward.

"Tuli. Please call me Tuli."

"I prefer *Boudi*."

"Why? Why won't you prefer Tuli? It's such a nice name."

Neil nodded, "*Dada* may not like it."

"Why wouldn't Soumen like it?"

"There are a number of rules about this house you've got to
understand." He felt another novel sensation of reconstructing his
principles. Somehow he felt he had to guard the honor of this house.
Tuli was oblivious to what he was thinking and felt scared.

"What rules?" Her face paled.

"Nothing." Neil smiled. And looked away. A peeping sense of
wanting to reassure her and understand her, popped its head beyond
all rules, principles and responsibilities of being loyal. And it felt
surprisingly pleasant.

Soumen walked in, in a white *kurta-pajama* and Neil quickly
said, "There! Your wait is over!"

Tuli turned to him and smiled. "Will you mind if Neil calls me
Tuli?" she asked as he sat down.

He looked at Neil, bewildered. Neil looked at him, flustered.

"No…why?"

"No, nothing. I was just pulling her leg. Manik, serve us food."

CHAPTER 12

Two days later Soumen joined back work. Tuli spent the day with the two children, Rumpa and Chompa, telling them stories of fairies and demons that kept them comfortably off the video games and kept them munching their food in a trance. Mahamaya liked it and said, "If you are going to tell them such wonderful stories they are going to bother you every day."

"I don't mind. I am not doing anything anyway."

Mahamaya cut in, "You are the eldest *bouma* (daughter-in-law) of the house. You should dress up properly after each phase of the day. Your mother has given you so much jewelry. You should wear them. Why have you taken off your bangles?"

"But I feel uneasy."

"You are a *Bouma*. You cannot afford to feel uneasy in anything. You have to get used to all this. And by evening I want to see you dressed in the best attire, perfume your room, make your bed and wait for Soumen in your bedroom."

That was the first time she had spoken to her at length and Tuli felt aghast! She felt she was being raped over and over again. She ran out of the dining hall and up the stairs into the terrace. She had to protect her soul.

Neil had gone to the University and his room was unlocked. Tuli walked into his room and closed the door. She felt better. Relieved and free. She switched on the computer and sat in front of it. She wanted to see Pamela Anderson once more.

A painting brush appeared on the screen. Damn! That creep! He's deleted Pamela with a picture of an idiotic brush painting a blue line. She waited for the hourglass to disappear. She didn't know where she would go from there. But she had the mouse and she would try out.

What didn't strike her then and struck her after a while of clicking on various files, that a 'painting brush' in Bengali meant 'TULI'!

She stopped shocked! A chill ran down her spine!! No, no she must be imagining things!

She quickly shut down the machine. The brush reappeared on the screen and the computer automatically shut down. She sat numb on the chair. Then switching off the computer she got off the chair and walked out onto the terrace. The day she met Neil up here she was wearing her favorite blue silk sari. She couldn't think straight. The March sun was high up and burning. She didn't feel like going downstairs to her room. She walked back into the cooler room and lay down on the bed. Then closed her eyes. She wanted to wipe out any impossible thoughts. The crazy boy, she thought mischievously. He must be having a crush on me!

She smiled.

And then she slept.

CHAPTER 13

Neil returned from university rather earlier than usual. His friends called him for a drag of hash, but he didn't feel like it. He wanted to get back home. He didn't know why.

He took a bus and rode back home. He usually never let anybody know he was back. He climbed the stairs right to the terrace into his room. He wanted to lie down though it was almost evening.

He walked in and saw the four kids playing in the courtyard. This was their playtime. He didn't disturb them. They didn't see him. He climbed onto the first floor and instinctively looked left at *Dada*'s room. The door was closed. Maybe Tuli was sleeping.

He didn't see Ma anywhere. Maybe she was in her room.

He wanted some tea. But he wanted more to be left alone. So he climbed up the stairs, quietly and fast.

He walked onto the terrace and saw Manik picking up the dried clothes. He asked him to send a cup of tea.

Manik was extremely intelligent and knew from the tone of his command that he was not in the right mood.

Neil walked into his room. Tuli was fast asleep on her stomach on his bed.

He was shocked! Doesn't anybody know she's up here? Obviously not, since her door was closed and like him, others thought she was inside the room.

Her hair was loose and strewn all over the pillow. She was in a green and white cotton sari, which carelessly uncovered her back and part of her les. They were white!

He looked away.

He kept his wallet and pen on the table and wondered what to do next. Wake her up? He turned around and took the liberty to watch her. She was in deep sleep and one hand was over her face. Despite that he could see the black eyes, the pouting nose and the small pink lips. The shimmering air from the fan made tufts of her hair shiver over her white cheeks.

He looked away again.

Dada is really lucky. He found himself saying that. And then he found his sanity. Why was she sleeping here? It's so hot up here. Then he assumed. Knowing her, she must have simply wandered off and found she was comfortable in this room.

He sat on the chair. He had to wake her up before Manik came with the tea. But she slept so peacefully he didn't have the heart to do so. She looked like a child.

He sighed and looked out of the window. Manik was coming towards him room with a cup of tea. Working on an instinct he walked out of his room, met him halfway and took the cup and saucer from his hands. He blocked Manik so that he couldn't see inside. He felt an innate urge to protect Tuli's honor, which could be at stake in this house even by this very normal action of hers.

He came back into his room.

"*Boudi*…" he called softly. "*Boudi*… want some tea?"

"Hmm.,." she woke up and quickly sat up. She crossed her brows and tried to fathom where she was. She rubbed her eyes and said, "Oh! I'm married."

Then she noticed Neil standing, "Hi!" she grouched.

"Want some tea?" Neil repeated. Her hair was wild and her face swollen from deep sleep.

"Hmm…" she nodded and took the cup from his hands. She sipped on the hot liquid readily.

Neil sat on the chair.

"Why are you sleeping here?" he asked leaning towards her.

"Hmm?" she looked up dazedly and then looked away, trying to think. "I don't know. Ma told me something I didn't like so I came up here and fell asleep. I think I was tired."

"So why didn't you sleep in your own room?"

Tuli frowned, wrinkled her nose and shook her head, "I don't like my room. I only make love there. I like it here."

Neil tried to ignore the sacrilegious remarks.

"But you know, people in this house may not like it."

She sipped her tea and looked up surprised, "Why?" "Because this is *my* room." His voice became a little cutting. He wanted to put some sense into her.

She thought a while. Then smiled, "You haven't had tea? You gave me your tea?"

Obviously the sarcasm hadn't registered inside her. He got angry.

"You didn't hear what I said? I said this was *my* room and you cannot sleep over here."

"Why? Are you that possessive about your room?" she fought like a child.

"Of course."

She smiled and tilted her head on one side, "I know you don't mean it. You're telling me all that to protect me."

Neil was flustered. He threw his hands in the air. "So if you understand everything, why are you going against the rule of this house? You'll get into trouble."

"I don't care what happens to me. I'm going to die anyway." She looked far away through the window. "But I'm sorry if I've hurt you. I don't want to put your honor at stake. It's okay, I'll never sleep in this room again."

She kept down her half-finished tea and walked out of the room. Neil felt terrible and called out, "*Boudi?*"

She stopped at the doorway. Neil walked up to her and stood very near. "You are an intelligent girl. But you have to be a little careful and understand the consequences of your actions. You know, you will be badly harmed."

She tilted her head in the same irresistible manner and looked into his eyes. He felt uncomfortable at the boring gaze, which seemed to look right into his inner self. She smiled and said sleepily and slowly, "You are a very nice person. You know… I like you."

She then turned and walked off. Neil saw her climbing down a different set of stairs that led to the back of the house. It's okay. She'll find her way.

He came back and felt restless. A series of different kinds of emotions swept over him. The foremost being a terrible urge to hold her and tell her that all was well. He blocked out the thought and tried to think rationally.

He paced up the room and picked up the half-finished tea. It was still hot. He sipped on it and felt better. He tried to analyze. It's okay. Whatever way he was trying to guard her was okay. But it was only making her place an inexplicable trust in him. Which is dangerous. He should look up to her as a sister-in-law and nothing else. *She was his sister-in-law.*

...But she seemed to know him so well. Trust him more than anybody did on this earth. Why? Is he worth it? He knew that her blasphemous and scandalous ways would put her in trouble in more ways than one. She hadn't met his aunts really. If she talked like that with them, they would dismiss her on the first day. And then *Dada* would be very angry. She may cause so much trouble — unknowingly, innocently. But she had more brains than one could imagine. So she'll sure use them. She had to. If she intended to survive in this house.

But the catch is that she never cared. So what's bothering him? Let her get into trouble. He'd simply close his room and stay away. Let *Dada* handle.

He realized that would be very difficult. But he had to do that. Stay away.

Tuli meanwhile had walked down the back stairs that led right into the wing in which her husband's aunts lived. The two teachers had come back from school and were leaning on the railing of the balcony, sipping tea and watching the kids playing downstairs. It was already time for them to come up and they were thinking about calling them up as soon as they finished their tea.

They noticed Tuli. She smiled and yawned, stretching her hands above her. They looked at her attire and her hair and assuming she was sleeping in Neil's room, looked in shock at each other.

Mahamaya was feeding the bird and watched the scene from the other end of the courtyard.

"*Bouma*," she called out. "Come here."

Tuli dawdled towards her. Mahamaya took her inside Tuli's room and made her sit on the bed.

She sat opposite her and asked, "You were sleeping in Neil's room?"

She nodded and smiled.

"Your room is so cool and nice. Why didn't you sleep here?"

"I know, I shouldn't have. Even Neil scolded me."

"He's back?" She was scared.

"Hmm. He's upstairs."

She tried to trust her son. "You see, you are a married woman. You shouldn't sleep in another man's room."

"But Neil isn't another man. He's my friend."

A warning bell rang immediately inside the elderly woman's mind on hearing the word 'friend'. She sensed a catastrophe and shuddered. She became very strict. "Don't disobey me. There are rules of the house you've got to obey. And now, put on a good *sari* and dress up. Stay in your room. Soumen will be back soon."

She smiled as though to tell her, that this was what she should be happy about and look forward to. And left.

Tuli sat, terribly disappointed.

She walked over to the bookshelf where she had arranged her favorite books that her mother sent, and took out *One Flew Over The Cuckoo's Nest*. She lay down on the bed and turned the pages. She couldn't read beyond a single line. She felt a clogging sense of claustrophobia and buried her head in the pillows and cried.

Soumen came back earlier than usual too. He rushed into the house and quickly informed Ma that he'd come. Then he rushed into his room to see Tuli.

She was lying on the bed on her face. A little callous in her dress than he imagined. He didn't mind. "Tuli?" he called out smiling.

She sat up. She was reading the book. She smiled back. "Hi, you're back? How's your day?"

He bolted the door. "Terrible! I missed you terribly." And got onto the bed. Her hair was scruffy and *sari* sloppily wound around. He wished she had been more attractively dressed. But he didn't want to waste any more time. He pulled her towards him and began kissing her vociferously.

"Oh! I missed you so much… I love you so much… " He whined and his hands moved.

Tuli remained flaccid and touched his hair, "Why don't you freshen up a bit?"

"I am freshening up. You are my intoxication." He felt the same throbbing pain in-between his legs.

She smiled and pulled away. "You're stinking. Please go and have a bath. Then I'll make love to you."

He felt his organ go limp.

CHAPTER 14

Tuli met the entire household for the first time in a week at the dinner table. It was a sixteen-seater oval, ornate table in mahogany with the chairs having velvet seats. Digambar Roy sat at the head of the table. His two brothers sat on either side and were a lot younger to him, maybe in their late and early forties. The next two chairs were for their respective wives, who sat with the *anchal* over their heads as a mark of respect for their elder brother-in-law and sister-in-law.

Digambar's two sons, Somu and Neilu sat on chairs opposite to each other. Beside Neilu sat the two teenage children, Sujoy and Neepa. At the tail end of the table sat Mahamaya, while Manik and Sumati, the two servants, served food.

Tuli's seat was set beside Soumen. She came into the hall dressed sloppily in the same *sari* she had worn after her bath in the morning. Her hair was wound in a slapdash bun and her eyes were sleepy and swollen. She didn't know anything about an *anchal* being on her head and sat down sleepy.

Neil looked up at her. She had been crying, he realized.

Mahamaya looked at her attire. She's a disobedient kid. I'll put it across to her mother when I next speak to her.

The eldest aunt looked at her attire. Good. She felt. All these years *Boudi* had dominated us into discipline. Now let's see what she does about her own daughter-in-law.

The youngest one looked at her. She's a rebel, she felt. I wish I could be like her. And she tried pushing off her *anchal* from her head a little, only unsuccessfully.

The three brothers talked business and seldom glanced at her side. The big man only felt Somu should take more care of her.

The other two brothers felt it was none of their business. *Dada* would manage everything.

Sujoy was fifteen and felt his *Boudi* was very pretty.

Neepa, 12, felt she wanted to grow up and be like her.

Soumen felt pleased that everyone was looking at his wife.

The object of their supervision was, however, almost asleep on her hands. What nobody realized was that she had made a controversial entry into the Roy family. Nobody realized. Least of all Tuli, herself. Her eyes were aching from crying. And she hated Neil sitting opposite her. She didn't want to look at him. She looked at Soumen instead and smiled and held his hand, inching closer to him.

The big man halted in mid-sentence at this view and everyone turned at her. She left his hand, her smile vanishing.

Neil looked down and tried to hide a smile. She was trying to make him jealous! She's crazy!

Dinner was served.

Midway through her mutton she looked at Soumen and spoke, "I want to go to college."

Her voice wasn't exactly a whisper and the entire family turned to her. She was in the middle of slurping on a big bone. But gave up the idea and looked around.

Soumen whispered, "But your mother said you didn't want to study further."

"But I'm bored!" She cried out in a whisper imitating him, which made the household turn towards her again.

Soumen was embarrassed. His mother was eating her fish item. She disliked mutton or chicken. She said, "Why don't you take a leave and take her out?"

"Leave? Ma, I took 20 days leave just a week ago. Baba will not like it."

"Then return home early and take her out. She needs time to settle down."

"I have so many backlogs. I can't return home before nine in the next few days." He stuffed some chapattis into his mouth. "Why doesn't Neil take her out?"

Neil looked up, his eyebrows raised.

"Yah, you come back from college at four-thirty at the latest. You can take *Boudi* out, can't you?" Soumen put it across in a tone that was rather underrating about whatever he was doing.

"No," Neil directly objected. "I don't have the time."

The other two ladies were enjoying the scene. Mahamaya saw that and reacted. She didn't want them laughing at her family.

"No Neilu, you shouldn't speak like that. She's your *Boudi*. Who else will she go with? And she only said that you were her 'friend'." She ended with an emphatic module on the last word.

Neil didn't like it. He felt trapped.

"Let's see," he said and looked at Tuli. She was chewing the bone, but there was a faint smile on her face.

CHAPTER 15

The next day Neil was awakened by a knock on his door at daybreak. It was still murky outside. He got up and opened the door. Tuli.

"Ooff," he said and threw himself back on the bed.

"Hey!" said Tuli, "Aren't we going out today?"

"Get lost!" He murmured.

She sat on the bed and pushed him, "Come on. Wake up. Look, the sun is coming up. It looks so wonderful.

"See I've finished my bath...

"See I smell so nice."

Neil snored.

"Come on, Neil," she caressed his hair and her voice softened. "Wake up."

Neil wasn't asleep. He just pretended to be. He felt an innate urge to put his head on her lap. Her lap was so near. He became stiff when she touched his hair.

Suddenly she pulled her hand back. He turned over and faced her. "What d'you want?" he said impolitely with his eyes closed.

She smiled. "Let's go. We got permission from Ma herself."

"Where?" he opened his eyes.

"We'll go to the lakes. I hear it's beautiful."

"You're mad!" He turned over.

Tuli hit at his back. "You promised it in front of everyone. Now look at you. Coward!"

He turned, "That hurts!"

"It was meant to be. Why won't you take me?"

She crossed her eyebrows and pouted her lips to feign crying.

Neil sat up. "Okay. But first get me a cup of tea."

She jumped up, her face lighting up instantly. "We'll have tea at a tea-stall. Come on, dress up. We'll take Soumen's bike. Look, I've even got the keys. Look, I'm wearing my shoes."

Neil slapped on his forehead with his hand. This girl is going to drive him crazy!

They left the house at five-thirty. Everyone was asleep. They pulled out the bike quietly and started it only after reaching the main road. Neil knew the nature of his family and asked the doorkeeper, Ram Singh, to just tell 'Ma' that they have gone out for a morning walk to a nearby park. The lakes were at the other end of the city. He didn't want to say that.

Tuli clung onto his stomach unabashedly once on the bike. "I should have worn my *churidars*. I could straddle the bike without holding you, so that you wouldn't feel ticklish."

"I am not feeling ticklish."

"I think I'll fall off. And die!" She screamed with her eyes closed as the bike picked up speed on empty roads.

"You'll not die! Not before having your baby."

Tuli freed her hands and raised them above her, "I'm flying. See Neil, I'm flying. I'm a bird!"

"Hold onto me, Tuli, you'll fall."

Tuli threw her head and laughed, "Ha ha, you finally called me Tuli."

"So? Does that change anything? You are still my *Boudi*."

"So what? You're my friend. That's more important."

She left him and sat bravely holding onto the backrest.

Neil suddenly accelerated his bike making Tuli yell falling back and clutching onto his stomach.

"What did you do that for?"

"So that you can hold me," he grinned.

Tuli hit him and then held him gently first. Then she wound her hand around his neck and put her chin on his shoulders. "You know something?"

"I don't know," he smiled.

"You're the best friend I've had in years!"

There was a slight tension when they returned home at eight o'clock. Soumen had woken up and on hearing this, though he didn't exactly like it, he calmed his slightly displeased mother by saying that he himself had asked them to go out together.

He remembered her in bed the night before. She wasn't in the mood. But he made her do wonderful things to him. He began humming a song as he entered the bathroom.

CHAPTER 16

Neil's university was on in full swing and he was barely at home after that day. He spent a lot of time with his friends smoking grass and hash. He simply wanted to return home late. He felt nervous about meeting Tuli.

She missed him desperately. She ran upstairs at dawn to find him gone for a jog which he had recently started. She met him sometimes hurrying through breakfast, where he barely spoke to her. She too kept quiet thinking he didn't want to speak to her. She catered to Soumen's needs instead.

Then one day she wanted to get it straight. It was a Friday and Neil was at home. He had slight temperature the evening before and Mahamaya was with him the whole morning. Tuli sulked in her room. In the afternoon, when the entire house was quiet, she found herself tiptoeing upstairs.

His door was closed. She pushed it. It was open. Neil was at the computer.

Tuli entered and sat down on the bed. Neil looked at her and then switched his attention back to the machine.

"Why don't you like me?" she came straight to the point.

"Hmm..?" Neil was thinking of an answer. He was forming a ploy that would make her simply hate him and love *Dada*.

"Is it my nose?" She was serious.

He turned and looked at her nose. "It looks perfect to me."

"I have reasonably good looks. I am slightly mad. That's it. Is that why you don't like me?"

He decided to give it straight. He turned. "Yes. I don't like you bothering me so much. I like to be left alone. Everybody hates it. You should realize you are hurting so many people."

She was too stunned to speak! Her eyes turned soulful and began brimming with sparks of water. She looked down. She couldn't speak.

Neil turned away. This was no time to hold her, cuddle her, kiss those tears away. *This was no time to tell her how much he…*

He aimlessly clicked on the mouse.

He heard soft sobs. He didn't turn. She spoke through a tear-choked voice.

"If you all hate me so much, I'll go away. I'll kill myself. I was to die anyway…"

Oh my God! Neil jerked himself up and rushed to her. He sat beside her and hugged her. She let out a wail!

"Come on… please don't cry… please don't cry…" He found himself kissing her on her cheeks. She was soaking his shirt with her tears. "Sweetheart… please sweetheart… you're such a sweetheart you don't know…" He kissed her closed eyes. She stopped crying and looked at him. Her face was a pool of tears… her eyes, cheeks, nose… Neil wiped her face off with his fingers.

"Listen," he held her face up. "You and me… we've become very close. So close, it's dangerous. You understand?"

She sniffed and shook her head. "But I love you."

Neil's world trembled. He remained calm for a minute. Then clicked his tongue. "I know that. That is why I am asking you to stay away. *Dada* is a very jealous man. It's not fair on him, too, right?"

"Let's run away," Tuli suggested sincerely.

He hid a smile and stroked her hair, "No. That's your idea. Not mine. I would like to see my family live in peace. Don't you see I compromise so much? You too have to compromise and stay away from me."

"I can't stay away from you," she wailed and new tears spurted forth from her eyes.

"Oh my god…" He kissed her lips lightly. "What am I going to do with you?"

"Marry me," She hugged him tight.

Neil laughed. "You forgot?"

"What?"

"You're married to my brother."

"Oh! I went to bed with him only a few times."

Neil pulled her back. "Tuli, are you for real, or do you play innocent?"

She suddenly became serious. "I play innocent." She stood up and wiped away her tears. Then stormed out of the room.

She was angry so suddenly that Neil didn't have time to react. Anyway, good for her, he felt. He threw himself onto his pillow and smiled.

And replayed the entire scene in his mind over and over again.

CHAPTER 17

April 1994

Tuli was bored!

All she did all day was take her food routinely, three times a day, play with the young children and talk to the two much-disciplined teenagers. They taught her not to be naughty and forbade her from opening the mynah's cage to let the bird free, which she often tried out.

They reprimanded her when she sat on the balcony railings or slipped down the staircase ones. They called her *'Boudi'* and refused to call her by her name, which she insisted considering the few years of age difference between them. They watched terrified when she climbed the banyan tree in their backyard and refused to join her up there when she called them. Mahamaya had a tough time tracking her throughout the day as she was forever missing. Mahamaya was thinking of simply giving up — trying to restrict her activities to more civilized ones like stitching and learning how to cook.

When the first April hurricane (the *Kalboishakhi*) struck one afternoon, Tuli ran out of her room, her hair open, up to the terrace. Sujoy and Neepa stared in horror as their *Boudi* summoned them from the terrace sitting on the high walls, her feet dangling over the open courtyard, two floors below! They looked at each other and were petrified about their *Jethima*, Mahamaya, who, accompanied by Manik, was running helter-skelter trying to shut the banging doors and windows, and wasn't even faintly aware of the cataclysm. Their mother and aunt had not yet returned home. So hadn't *Chhorda*. They began waving their hands at her frantically asking her to get down — when Neil entered.

Seeing *Chhorda*, the two children ran inside. Neil got a bit perplexed and followed their eyes assuming they were looking at something in the sky.

And then he saw her!

He was horrified and instantly ran up to the terrace.

A clamor of thick air overtook him completely the moment he stepped onto the terrace. A wild wind, filled with dust that twisted into a vortex of air currents, danced like a fierce tornado. Trees swayed vociferously against an ashen sky and the hoardings on top of buildings shuddered threateningly. Stunning white streaks of light slashed across the sky, which darkened every second, camouflaging the earth into submitting to its wild desire to annihilate it completely. The hurricane danced on the terrace to and fro, putting Neil completely off-balance.

He shaded his eyes from the dust and saw Tuli. An unnerving bundle of challenge — sitting in a bright orange *sari*, the *anchal* of which flew like a blazing fire. She sat solemnly on the wall, unperturbed, lost in thoughts, oblivious to the gyrating madness around her.

He didn't want to call out to her and scare her. She'd fall. Fall from the second floor down into the courtyard. He quietly walked towards her and held her hand.

"Come," he quietly beckoned.

She turned and looked at him. He was in his favorite blue T-shirt and jeans. She didn't smile. She simply looked at him. Her eyes boring into his despite the hurricane cutting in between them.

He tugged at her. "Come down," he said. She remained unmoved — a challenging look in her eyes that spoke so many unsaid things. It said, *Why are you bothering me?* It said, *Don't come near me, I might love you.*

Neil looked away. "Come on," he said.

Then suddenly the big drops fell. The heavens tearing apart, water rushing down from it intending to inundate the earth and obliterate it completely.

He extended his hands and held her underneath her arms like he would hold a child. And pulled her off the wall onto hard ground. The rains began drenching them entirely. He caught her hand and ran for cover towards his room. Tuli ran along. Then on reaching the room, she suddenly wrenched her hand free and ran in the opposite direction, towards the stairs. Neil stood at the door, watching her, getting wet. Tuli stood at the stairway and turned. She cringed her eyes through the thick curtain of rain and waited. Then suddenly she ran back, her feet slipping — into his arms.

She wound her hands around his neck and buried her face in his T-shirt, as he took her inside. Fire was burning inside despite the incessant water outside. He slowly bolted the door with her clinging onto him. And then the window.

The water raged outside with interrupted clasps of thunder shattering the universe. And fire raged inside. They flung themselves onto the small bed and he began kissing her tenderly. She gave in slowly, gently. Neil had never made love to anyone before and his hands quivered. He paused after each step and looked into her eyes, waiting for her to say 'Stop'. But she was *Kalboishakhi* personified and tears of blocked emotion streamed down her eyes. She loved him hopelessly, wanted him indefatigably, wanted to run, fly anywhere away with him, far from reality. She suddenly realized all that and cried choking with the emotion. Neil stopped midway and looked up to her.

"What happened?" he pulled himself up and caressed her face.

She opened her eyes and threw her hands around him, making him bury his face in her bare breasts.

"I love you," she could manage to say. "I love you so much…" she cried like a baby.

Neil looked up. And kissed her. He wanted her to become an inseparable limb of his. Never wanting to let her go. His passion burst forth in spurts as though he wanted to take revenge on God for not giving him Tuli. And then he became a poet and was writing a beautiful poetry, playing a soothing harp. And then suddenly he was a ravaging devil, equated with the mood outside, wheedling out her sanity, as if punishing her for punishing him.

Tuli was like a piano, on which he played a pitiless symphony, a neurotic orchestra — submitting completely to his feverish passion. Her own temperature ascended until it reached the crescendo. She felt numb with the fire that danced through her. She never knew such an inferno existed in her until then, which was burning her from head to toe.

The storm raged for an hour outside. When it stopped it had become dark.

She slept naked. Neil lit a cigarette, sitting naked beside her. He was suddenly apprehensive. She was missing from downstairs for over an hour. He put on his jeans and the T-shirt that was thrown wildly on the floor and went outside, closing the door behind him. He crossed the terrace and looked down from the boundary walls bordering the courtyard. No one was around. The corridor and the courtyard below were watery. Everything smelt of fresh earth.

Taking a wild risk of leaving Tuli sleeping nude in a room with an unlocked door, he quietly raced downstairs.

He quickly saw around. And found the three ladies huddled inside the huge kitchen, sipping tea. Manik was cutting vegetables.

They spotted Neil. "You've come?" asked his mother. "Want something to eat? Got drenched?"

He sensed they hadn't a clue. Ma hadn't guessed that he came from upstairs and not downstairs. They hadn't missed Tuli either. But how could that be? Her room was simply shut and not locked.

He tried out something. "Is *Boudi* still sleeping?" he put in rather casually.

Then he got the confirmation.

His mother became very quiet. Then said casually, keeping the other two ladies' eager ears in mind, "I keep telling her not to. But it seems she likes your room very much. She must be up there. Neil please send her down. I'll engage her in some household work."

Neil heaved a sigh. He turned to race back upstairs and saw Sujoy standing against the railing and looking at him. Neil's heart leapt. Sujoy was a witness. He paused a while and then walked across to him.

"Hi!" he smiled.

Sujoy was old enough. Neil sensed he understood something.

He said in a low voice, "See the rains? Your *Boudi* and I were sitting on the stairs and watching the rains. It was so scary! Why didn't you come up and join in the fun?"

Sujoy looked up at him and simply said, "I did." Then he slowly walked off with his head down.

Neil raced upstairs. Sujoy was old enough. But knowing how much he loved him, he wouldn't let him down. *He hoped!*

Tuli was oblivious to all the tensions and slept naked under the fan, a little curled up, from the growing chill around. Neil felt she might catch a cold and pulled the covers over her. Then he closed the door and held her tight. *"If I have to face a raging society outside for her, I will."* He promised silently and kissed her cheeks.

Instinctively she wiped it off. He kissed her again. This time she opened her eyes. She seemed to be a little surprised to see him. And then she remembered everything. She threw her hands around him.

"Wake up sweetie-pie, the world's raging downstairs."

She sat up with a jerk and the covers fell off from her breasts. Neil caressed one and bent to kiss the other.

"Don't!" she pushed him away. "Don't make me go so mad." She smiled and pulled back the covers.

"Get dressed fast. People want you downstairs. Everybody knows," he said solemnly.

"What?" her mouth fell open.

"You've committed a sin. Won't you get punished for it? Ma is standing downstairs with a whip."

"What rubbish!" she finally understood. "I have committed a sin? What about you? Isn't a *Boudi* supposed to be like a mother?"

Neil folded his hands, "Okay, my mom," and then cupped her face in his hands, "Now get dressed."

That day at dinner Neil whispered to Sujoy seated beside him, "Can we have a man to man talk today?"

Sujoy looked up. A little scared. Then nodded.

"Good. Then after dinner bring some English problem upstairs. I have a surprise for you." He glanced at Tuli. She was busy whispering something to Soumen and giggling. Soumen too laughed and said something in her ear at which she gave a dry smile, turned to Neil and winked at him.

They both instantly looked at Mahamaya. She hadn't noticed. Tuli then looked at Neepa and Sujoy, who had noticed, and raised her eyebrows at them as if to say "What?" They shook their heads quickly. Tuli leant back, hiding behind Soumen, made a pout and tapped her lips with her fingers. `No talking in this house'.

Sujoy came up after dinner. He stood at the door.

"Come in," said Neil. "Sit down."

He sat down.

Neil lit a cigarette and passed it to him. He looked up surprised.

"Come on, try a puff. It doesn't harm to be a little naughty."

"No, Ma will smell."

"She won't. One puff won't smell."

Sujoy took a puff and coughed. He gave it back to Neil.

"Okay, now you are an adult. We can talk. You see, often certain things are beyond even your *Chhorda*'s control. Often adults commit a mistake which they think is only right." He paused. "You understand what I mean?"

The teenaged boy nodded. He was slightly confused.

Neil continued, "When you grow up, you'll also sometimes do certain things which your brain tells you not to and your heart tells you to. We are human beings; and not God. And that is why we operate on our heart's desires."

Sujoy looked up and simply said, "I like *Boudi* very much."

Neil realized he understood. "I know that. And keep in mind that she loves you four the most in this house."

"Yes, she plays with us. She's a wonderful person."

"So, if you think she's done something wrong will you forgive her?"

He smiled, "Yes."

"Good. Now don't think about anything. Your *Chhorda* will take care of everything."

He nodded.

Neil kissed his forehead. "Love you very much. Now go quickly. And don't tell anyone about this."

"I won't. I promise." He got up and walked towards the door. Then he stood there and looked back, "I love you very much," he said solemnly. His *Chhorda* had taught him to say this to all those who he had loved.

CHAPTER 18

Soumen was interested in good sex, good money and good drinks. In that order. He had married a weird person. She's wonderful in bed whenever she's in a mood. She drove him wild. They often had two to three go'-s in a single night. She seemed to be insatiable. And such a white skin and such an incredible figure! He often felt like videotaping her on those wild nights and then playing them later on, watching them in his office whenever he missed her badly. However, on occasions like the times recently, she became limp as a piece of mutton in bed.

He never did mind. He knew that once he gave her really good attention he'd get her just the way he wanted. He knew she and Neil were getting a little too close. That's okay. He was a broad-minded person. And nobody really complained.

As long as she was in a good mood.

She had to be in a good mood. She always needed foreplay. Then she always tried out something new. Sometimes she was submissive as a lamb. Sometimes a raging wild tigress, clawing him out of his senses. The other day she submitted so much that she told Soumen to hit her and rape her. She kept moving away from him. And he caught her by the hair and hit her. She moaned and knelt in front of him.

His pants became tight and he wanted to rush back home.

He couldn't. He had a pile of files in front of him. He did the thing he could. He went into the bathroom and masturbated.

CHAPTER 19

June 1994

More than a month had passed since the *Kalboishakhi* hurricane. Soumen had no objection in Tuli learning to use the computer from Neil. Even Mahamaya felt that her unconventional energies could be channelized properly and she would do less harm to the four growing children. She was forever up to mischief and distracting them from their routines. She was teaching them bizarre things. How to catch a spider live or climb down on to the balcony portico. She was teaching them how to climb a tree and slide down the staircase railings. Mahamaya forgot how to take a short nap peacefully on afternoons. The other day she caught her sitting on the balcony portico, munching *aachar* — a sour and salty concoction usually made from the seasonal vegetables — dangling her legs over the courtyard. One day they were studying in the evening and she left a live cockroach on their table. She was getting tired of scolding her.

The kids were picking up the mischief fast and their mothers complained.

One day Mahamaya found her squatting on the *roak* [26] and sifting through some papers, which their doorkeeper, Ram Singh was showing her. She was very serious and didn't come up immediately when Mahamaya called her. When she did come up, rather ran upstairs, (she always ran up the stairs taking two to three at a time and jumped down the last four steps when climbing down), whistling, (Mahamaya was shocked again) and when her mother-in-law asked her, "What were you doing with Ram Singh?" she said with her eyes wide open. "You know, he had been duped of his properties in Bihar by his brothers. But I think there is still a way out. I think…"

"Why don't you listen to some music or watch TV in your room?" Her mother-in-law cut in rather rudely.

Tuli stopped. "But I don't like TV."

"Then read books. Listen to music. No *Bouma* of our house sits on the *roak* with the *durwan* [127] during the late afternoon. Is that clear?"

Tuli made a face. "Even Neil's not back. Can I go and operate the computer in his room?"

"Okay," said the elderly lady and walked off. It was a better option.

Then one day she smelt tobacco and peeped to see her smoking *bidi*, hiding behind the *thakurdalan,* while Sujoy sat beside her!

She was shocked! She didn't know how to react! What a horrible mess! Her mother had really dumped the girl on them. Why didn't she tell her all these? Now what should she do? Perform a *Satyanarayan puja* [128]? Call an *ojha* [129]? Hit her? Scold her? Or pray?

But she knew one thing. She shouldn't let Soumen know about this. He had a horrible temper and would scream and shout. The other two women were waiting for an opportunity like this to break up the family and the business.

Neil was a saner person. She decided to speak to him. Maybe he'd drive some sense in her. She called him aside after he came back and let out. "Neilu, I don't know what to do with your *Boudi*…"

"Why? What happened?"

"She was smoking *bidi*." She paused for his reaction. He had none. "I think she got it from Ram Singh. What a shame!" She was almost in tears.

Neil held her and comforted her. "Don't be upset. Where is she? I'll speak to her." Then as an afterthought he added, "I think she needs to go to college. She should do something constructive with her time."

"Do anything." His mother was desperate. "Get her admitted into a college. But see that she doesn't bring a bad name for the family.

And don't tell your *Dada*. He wouldn't understand." She added, "She's in your room. Please try to make her understand."

Neil leapt up the stairs. He was angry, very angry with her. How could she be so callous and not take anyone's feelings into consideration?

He burst in.

Tuli looked up from the machine as she saw him and leapt forward to hug him. "I missed you so much the whole day. I love you so much…"

Neil pushed her back. Her face paled.

"You've been smoking *bidi*?"

Her face turned ashen.

"Where did you get it from? Ram Singh?"

She mumbled, "Yes…"

"Ram Singh gave you *bidi* and you *took* it?"

"No," she said solemnly, "he didn't give it to me. I stole one from his case."

"*Stole!…Why?*" Neil was exasperated and sat down on the bed.

"I wanted to try it out," she murmured.

"You wanted to *try* out *bidi*? You know Ma saw you?"

She gasped. "Now what will happen?"

"She'll send you back to your mother's place and never get you back. She'll get *Dada* married again."

She broke into tears. "I can't stay away from you…" She sat down on the bed beside him.

Despite the tension Neil smiled. She was incorrigible and loved him so much. She didn't have any problems about her husband getting married again. But she had problems leaving him!

He looked at her and smiled. Her face instantly lit up. She smiled and hugged him. Then kissed him on his cheeks. He sighed and pushed her away. No. He was getting too weak. He had to think straight…

…He wanted to run away with her out of this world…

"Sit down at the computer. Let's see what you've learnt."

She sat down on the chair like an obedient student.

"Open a new file."

She clicked on 'New'.

"Now give it a name."

She instantly typed 'Neil'.

He nodded his head and deleted the name. "Type Tuli."

"What's wrong with 'Neil'?"

"It's your file, so it should have your name. Type TULI."

She typed 'AAKASH'.

"Who's that?" He asked bewildered.

"My son." She smiled contentedly.

"Get lost! You'll never learn anything." He stood up and paced the room.

"All you're interested in is me, and how to malign the family name …" He knew he was being unfair. But that was the only way to make her go back to her husband.

Tuli looked at him hurt. Her face pale. He didn't bother. "What do you think of yourself? You are that irresistible that any man would be drawn to you?"

She frowned as she looked down. And then left everything and ran out of the room.

Neil sat down exasperated. He felt restless. He had to decide on something before the matter went out of his hands. He had two more years at the University before he could take up a professional career. A job, to be able to support himself. To get out of this house. Maybe, he should try to get a PG accommodation. He looked around his room. He loved it so much. It's okay, I can come back anytime to spend weekends, he thought. Maybe by that time she'll settle down with *Dada* and get over me. *Will I get over her?* Of course. I'll date a million girls in college. I'm sure I'll find somebody suited to my imaginations. *Tuli is beyond my imaginations!* She's a firebrand. A hallucination… illusory. A phoenix bird… jets of a tornado… a dart of lightning… an anarchist! An avant-garde rebel in an archaic get up. I am a person who *confronts* social norms. *She doesn't even know they exist!*

She's at the wrong place with the wrong man. If her energies were channelized rightly, with guidance and wisdom, she could become a success. But was that attuned to this family's set of laws? A *Bouma* of the house — a roaring success in a man's world? In India, a woman's home is at her in-laws'. Her identity is that of her in-laws'.

What can she do without them? So many people were involved if her existence was ever tried to be advocated. Neil himself could steer her and propel her to success. But would he be able to get out of that after that? He loved her so much. He held his head. *God!* I never knew that love could be such a throbbing emotion... such a slashing pain... such a magnetic attraction that all senses went flaccid, beyond repair...

No! He had to be in his senses. Okay. Take one step at a time. Get her admitted into a college. He decided he had to talk to his brother that evening.

Tuli didn't come for dinner that evening. When Mahamaya asked Soumen her whereabouts, he said she had a stomach ache and wouldn't eat. Neil understood why she didn't want to eat. He wanted to go to her and make up. But he didn't do that.

He sat opposite Soumen and brought up the topic, "Ma was saying if Tuli could go to college. You know, she spends the entire day idling and fiddles with my computer." He made it sound like a complaint. He didn't want Soumen to sense anything. "She is also up to a lot of mischief." He looked at his mother for her espousal.

"Yes," added Mahamaya . "I think you can enroll her in BA classes."

"Okay," said Soumen, "Neil, tomorrow you go and get her admitted. I think classes have started. If you think I need to speak to anyone, I will."

It was decided.

Soumen came back after dinner and found Tuli lying down in the same way. She was hungry, but she wanted Neil to come and get her. He didn't. She was more upset now.

"Tulip, my Tulip," Soumen climbed on the bed, "I've got good news for you. You are going to college. Do you have your mark sheets?"

She was not as thrilled as he thought she would be. But she camouflaged it aptly. She sat up. "No, they are in Katoa."

"Then tomorrow you go with Neil to Katoa. You'll see your mother too, and get the mark sheets. Then we can get you admitted, okay?"

She nodded. Okay, so she was going to Katoa. One good news. And with Neil! She was ecstatic!

"I'll go and tell him this." She jumped out of the bed.

Soumen said, "He knows. Just tell him to go with you to Katoa. But come down fast. " He smiled mischievously.

Tuli ran out of the room. Up the stairs. Into his room.

He was not there. She came out and found him standing by the terrace boundary wall looking at the street below, smoking.

She crept up to him and hit him from behind. "HOAH!" she tried to scare him. He jumped. Then turned his attention back to the street below.

"Tomorrow you are taking me to Katoa. We'll stay over there for a day and I'll get my mark sheets," she beamed.

"Who decided that?"

"Soumen."

"I have important classes tomorrow. I can't go."

Her face fell. She looked at him with hurt eyes.

"Don't look at me like that. It won't change a thing."

"I am not bothering you anymore. I'll get into a college and then I'll not trouble you at all."

"Oh yeah? Your college runs for twenty-four hours?"

"No, but then I'll be studying and busy. I won't even come up here."

Neil gave in. He couldn't hold back anymore. He had hurt her too much. And he was equally at fault. He held out his hands and pulled her towards him. Then lifted her face and held it.

"I'm sorry I hurt you so much," he whispered. "I love you so much, I don't know what to do with you..." He committed for the first time and Tuli's eyes shot open with elation. She crept up to him and kissed him on his lips. And then he held her and threw the cigarette away and kissed her fervently. She whispered, "Let's go in."

"No!" Neil pushed her away. "*Dada* is waiting for you."

"But I want to sleep with you."

"Get lost!" Neil blushed at her candor, nervous with his own emotion.

She suddenly turned serious, "Neil, one day I'll get so lost that you'll never find me again, anywhere."

"Don't say that," he remembered the prediction about her and felt a clamp in his throat. He pulled her into his arms and said, "Don't say that again."

He pulled her out and said, "Go now. Tomorrow morning we'll go to Katoa. And before that," he patted her lips with his fingers, "Eat some biscuits. You're hungry, aren't you?"

Tuli threw her arms around him and kissed him on his neck. "I love you," She smiled and left.

He felt something she mentioned, repeating at the back of his mind.

CHAPTER 20

Katoa, June 20 1994

Katoa was a small town in the Burdwan district of West Bengal, one hundred and sixty-two kilometers away from Calcutta at the banks of a tributary of the Ganges, Ajay River. Tuli had lived her entire life there. But today she was going back there as a 'guest'.

That was the rule. After marriage, the girl is treated as a guest when she comes back to her father's house, be it a day after the marriage, be it a lot later. Her home — where she was born, saw the light of the universe for the first time and grew up believing this was her den —transforms overnight into a 'house' for her to visit. Her parents, whose creation she is, treats her 'well', as though she belonged to someone else. She is expected to instantly take on her in-laws as her own parents and treat her own parents as someone she knew very well and cared for. This phenomenon, technically, should take a long time to shape in a girl's mind before she should understand that the society expected her to change into a woman from a girl, and a protector from the protected, overnight. Usually the *fright* of a rejection from both ends makes her fluid enough to accept this rule and accommodate her existence within a short time.

Tuli never knew what *fear* was all about. So for her... *she was simply going home!*

She glowed visibly and leaning on Neil's shoulders, pointed out excitedly at the rice fields and the names of villages and towns, on their way in the local train, as if he was seeing them for the first time.

"Excuse me," said Neil when she pointed at a colorful bird, saying it was a kingfisher, "I know what a kingfisher is."

Tuli blushed, "No, I thought there were no birds in the city."

The man sitting opposite them was enjoying their conversation. As Neil's eyes fell on him, he bared his betel-leaf smeared teeth, "Newly weds?"

Neil looked stunned as he looked for the right reply. Tuli nodded shyly beside him. Neil looked at her and then out of the window.

He wasn't ready to give answers about their relationship yet.

They reached Katoa near noon. Tuli's uncle was standing beside the collapsible iron gates of the station where the ticket collector checked the tickets. Tuli ignored the black-attired collector who took out his hand trying to stop her, saying "Ticket?" and ran out of the gate to hug her uncle. The man, in his late fifties, too was beaming. Neil handed the ticket to the confused collector and walked out.

"Welcome to Katoa, Neil," said Partho Nagchowdhury. Neil bent to touch his feet. Partho instantly hauled him up and hugged him. "This is better," he smiled at Neil.

The latter suddenly knew where Tuli inherited her *freshness* from.

"Let's take two rickshaws," Partho said after stepping into the sunlight out of the station.

Tuli gleamed and never stopped smiling. She looked at Neil for every reaction of his. "I'll take you to the Ajay River today evening." She wanted Neil to like the place. She wanted him to like her kin. Tuli and Neil got on to one rickshaw and her uncle in another, with the luggage.

The touches of city life, consisting of telephone booths, computer centers, Xerox copy shops and fast-food joints, that sporadically tried to impress a stray traveler, faded instantly as they went round a bend into the heart of the town. The arena turned somber with stately houses — their ages dating back a few hundred years — lining up on both sides of narrow lanes. The main entrance of most of the houses had chunky doors with large iron rings for handles. The windows had wrought-iron railings and half-curtains for privacy. The *roak* was common to all dwellings and Neil found they were mirroring a few exceptional features. Groups of boys, simple faces... fervent idealists, were sitting on them. Old men, who were not yet written off as they were in the city, huddled together, talking of their 'future'. Little toddlers played, with no fear of rash traffic. No one was afraid. There was hope all around, as a matter-of-fact. Idealism ruled. No one was in a hurry to prove a thing.

Neil realized from where Tuli got her *strength*.

Every single person's face beamed when they saw Tuli and heads turned as they passed by. They probably thought him to be her husband, and he felt abashed.

"You are angry?" Tuli looked at him. She had noticed the coiled abashed look in his eyes. Neil nodded and smiled at her, "Your town is beautiful," he said, assuring.

She wasn't assured. And her eyes said so. Her uncle in the rickshaw behind them wished to everyone cheerfully informing each of them that her niece had come.

Neil felt out of place.

The two rickshaws came to a halt in front of another grand looking building. This one was a little in shambles. The facade was painted in yellow, rather inexpertly, which carelessly covered the flamboyant motifs above the portal. The door was painted a repelling dark green, probably in anticipation of it getting dirty soon.

The initial euphoria of personal happiness, permeating into a sense of responsibility that Neil felt, of substituting his brother to take Tuli back home for a purpose, soon merged into a sense of guilt, as he suddenly felt he was treading on Soumen's territory. The sense of guilt — that he so long had denied with reasoning — suddenly irked him. There were certain things 'to-be' and 'not-to-be'. He was performing the art of 'not-to-be' and was supporting it with logic. What was so easy to bargain-for in the city, became very difficult in this land of 'taking relationships by their face value. He hated himself for accompanying her.

"Wait here a second," said Tuli's uncle and rushed inside. "Where is everybody? They've come." He announced inside.

Instantly there was a clamor and the sound of conch-shells filled up the air.

Neil wanted to disappear.

Tuli's mother, Srimati, came out in a white *sari*. Neil remembered she was a widow. Weren't widows supposed to be absent during an auspicious household moment? Neil remembered something like that being mentioned in his own home. He didn't remember the rest. Obviously this was not the rule here.

He understood why Tuli was such a *non-conformist*.

Srimati had a plate in her hands with a burning lamp on it, a few flowers, grains of paddy and tiny sprouts of grass — all of which were considered holy. Two other women, one in a white *sari* like hers and one in a red-bordered white *sari* blew conch-shells beside her.

Neil stood a step behind Tuli. She pulled him beside her. Srimati circled the plate three times in the air in front of them and smeared small red dots on their forehead. Then she sprinkled the paddy grains and welcomed them inside.

Tuli bent to touch her feet, but her mother was in tears. She pulled her up and hugged her. They hugged tight for a few moments and Tuli burst into tears. Everyone around them sniffed their noses. They were all trying to hide their emotions.

Neil looked around. The entire household was downstairs and they all looked at Neil. They all knew Neil was to come and not Soumen, as was informed by Mahamaya over the phone.

Tuli separated from her mother and pulled at him. "Ma, this is Neil." He touched the elderly lady's feet. She held his forehead and kissed him on it. "Live long, my son, be happy."

A faint surge of welcoming reassurance filled into Neil's soul and he stopped feeling so guilty now.

He was put up in Damayanti's room, which was practically unused. It had a bed, a cupboard, a table and a chair. *Chhotoma's* bookshelf was the only thing in the house that was locked and this piece of history fitted itself into this room. The shelves housed a hundred books, ranging from Tagore to Shakespeare, from Da Vinci's paintings to unknown artists' works, from astronomy to palmistry. Neil looked at the collection and was envious. Someone here read a lot, he assumed.

He kept his bag and stepped out of the room. The house had a similar concept of a courtyard, which, however, was more dissipated. Maybe because it was without the *thakurdalan*. The courtyard had a balcony running around it and rooms lined up along the corridor, like their own. However, *something was amiss*.

The railings were broken in places and painted new in others. One part of the first floor was in complete wreck. Two rooms were locked and the walls were almost disintegrating. An empty wooden birdcage swung in the breeze at the other end.

He smiled. Tuli must have set the bird free. The floor was clean but the railings were dusty as clothes-lines ran above him haywire. The wooden, ornate porticos were disintegrating in parts, eaten by borers and painted in an incomprehensible black oil paint. His room's door had new curtains; the other doors had old ones.

It was a jaunty setup, a rakish ambience where conformity was an offhand idea. People were more self-indulgent, more of throwing caution to the wind. Neil felt a surprising relaxation. Nothing was in place. Nothing had a rule. Nothing was in compliance to the regulations of running a successful household. Yet everything was in such synergy. Everyone loved one another so much. Everyone was so happy.

Neil learnt from where Tuli inherited her *mayhem*.

He came back into his room. The room was tidy — in fact, very tidy. He realized this had been the prime job of the household once their advent was announced. He deciphered, all these came from the heart. They all loved Tuli and hence loved anybody even faintly acquainted with her.

A new mat was placed near the doorway. New curtains hung from freshly dusted windows. One small rack was emptied in a hurry where he figured he had to keep his clothes, if needed. A circular marble-top wooden table, with intricate wooden works running halfway down to the floor from its sides, spoke a lot of the family's heritage, even if its 'present' refused to acknowledge such veneration as reality. The table was complemented with an equally ornate, heavier, armchair. The table had a white lattice tablecloth spread on it, that couldn't hide its beauty.

A green bed sheet was spread over a single bed, complimentary to the greenery outside. He noticed the foliage and walked over to the window. A picturesque village greeted him. A thick maze of green soothed his eyes. A big pond below shimmered in the overhead sun below as four ducks waded calmly.

"May I come in?"

Neil turned and saw a petite girl standing at the door, peeping through the curtains. She was as frail and pretty as Tuli. She wore a peach colored cotton *sari* and white cotton blouse. Her hair was neatly plaited and she wore no spec of makeup. She had a cup and saucer in one hand and a plate of sweets in the other.

He smiled at her, "Yes, please."

She smiled and walked inside. She placed the plates on the table and said, "I'm Hansi. Tuli's cousin."

Neil smiled at her. 'Hansi' meant 'smile'. He looked at the plate. Eight oversized *rasogolla*s adorned the white china. The cup of tea looked enticing.

"I won't be able to eat so many. I'll have one."

He picked up one *rasogolla*, a sweet made from curdled milk dipped in sugar syrup, and popped it into his mouth. The Bengali delicacy melted in his mouth.

He picked up the cup of tea. "That's all. Thanks."

"You're sure?" Hansi asked, wide-eyed — the same innocent wide-eyed look.

Neil nodded.

She never insisted. She picked up the plate, smiled and left.

Neil put the cup on the table and lit a cigarette. Then with the burning roll stuck between the first two fingers of his left hand, he picked up the saucer and plate and walked over to the window. A woman was bathing in the pond. Following an initial instinct, he looked away. Then he let his eyes wander.

The woman had all her clothes on and was smearing water on her body with her hands. She had a comfortably voluptuous body and having no knowledge that anybody could be watching her, made no attempts to conceal it. She dipped her head into the water twice and then sat on the banks, simply wading in the water.

Somehow, Neil never found the visual obscene — at best, sexy. The entire appeal was so innocent that he found it easier to identify the woman as his sister, sister-in-law or aunt at best. That entire sycophantic obsession about sex back in the city merged into something very pure and humane. She was somebody's mother, sister, aunt, wife or daughter. He earlier had a trying time keeping these definitions alive. But here his conviction was confirmed so easily.

He suddenly thought of Tuli. And found he blamed himself for the entire relationship.

CHAPTER 21

July and August, 1994

Tuli got enrolled for Arts graduation in a girls' college nearby. No co-education for her and not going far off. She was to leave for college in their family car and come back by car. So, no straying. A sense of anticipation was creeping up Soumen's mind about her immense attachment to his brother. He believed they were brotherly — at worst, friendly. But something at the back of his mind told him to be wary.

He had hated his brother. He was an ace at camouflaging it. But he often had wished Neil wasn't born at all. From childhood Ma had been partial to her younger son and took up his side. Soumen was a quiet child and never argued. He simply took it out on his brother by tearing off his favorite comic book or breaking his pencil. He always did these things quietly and nobody ever found out. Then Ma blamed Neil for being so careless and he got the scolding. Soumen felt Neil knew who did them but never put him in trouble. That, however, didn't change his attitude towards him. All his life Neil was preferred by all his relatives and his opinion taken in family decisions. Neil was always the delicate one, small and physically weak and hence, pampered by all. They often ignored Soumen for his condescending attitude. He never forgot or forgave a hurt in a hurry. His mountain-high hatred for his brother accentuated with Tuli's increasing attachment to him. So he decided to nip this in the bud.

So he caged Tuli.

For days Tuli never got to be with Neil. Soumen had become very demanding of late and woke up very early. He asked her to join him for tea, iron his clothes and told her smilingly how much he would like it if she prepared his breakfast. Then he would make her hang around him until he left for office.

"I am becoming so dependent on you," he smiled at her and hugged her.

She had to get ready for college immediately after he left and barely saw Neil brushing past her leaving for his University. She stopped him one day and asked him to come with her in the car. He refused rudely and went off.

Even after returning from college, she hardly got to see him. Mahamaya gave her some chores to finish in the kitchen or asked her to prepare a dish for dinner. Neil was just a floor away, but it seemed everybody was chaining her down slowly, keeping her away from Neil.

She began feeling claustrophobic and one evening decided to duck all chores.

Mahamaya had gone to visit a relative and would not be back before dinner. She had assigned her to prepare a dish for dinner and then study. She made the dinner fast and by early evening, she was running frantically up the stairs.

He was studying.

She closed the door and bolted it. Neil looked at her surprised.

"What do you want?" he asked rudely.

"I want to run away." She sat down on the bed and said somberly.

"Why? Did anybody scold you?"

"No, they are all keeping me away from you."

"But I don't want to see you."

"Why?" She was in tears.

"Look Tuli, grow up, okay? If you don't stay away from me I'll have to shift to a paying guest accommodation."

She looked at him, hurt. One big tear fell from her eyes.

The she spoke. She spoke like a matured woman. Like a wise person.

"I know I had been troubling you all a lot. I was married to your brother and naturally took you as my brother-in-law. But you are such a wonderful person, I fell in love with you. Not Soumen. Soumen never understands me the way you do. He is only interested in taking me to bed. I know I have a good figure and he gets turned on by it. But I have a heart and a mind that's even more fascinating. He never tried to understand them. You did. I didn't plan to fall in love with you. I simply did. Now if I can't come near you, I'll escape." She looked up. A scary look in her eyes. "Somehow."

Neil listened to her astounded. She spoke the truth so unabashedly. She was a mature person inside and knew what she was doing. All this while Neil thought she was a kid and simply followed her hearts' desire. But now he realized she was a woman. A woman, whose emotional needs are not fulfilled by her husband. He had unconsciously fulfilled them. He looked out of the window into the starry night above. Winter was four months away, but a chill filled the air.

He looked at her. She was lost faraway in thoughts. Her big, black eyes angry and hating the world. The dim light of the table lamp made her look ominous. It looked as if she could get up and do anything from that point.

What would happen if I made love to her now?

He was shocked at his thoughts! Was he only attracted to her physically? No. Never, he smiled. He had never seen such a wildfire, a hurricane, all his life. I think I fell in love with her the day she told me she smoked, so unassumingly. I knew she had an inferno inside. I perhaps ignited it.

He looked at her, at a complete loss for words. He felt a clamp in his throat and, despite the threats that his mind made on his heart of abandoning support whatsoever, he did exactly what his heart told him to do.

They made love for a shorter time, considering the risk they were taking. All the while they essentially clutched onto each other as if never to let go of each other. They laughed and cried. In happiness and in pain, as he kissed her all over. They jested about their existence and thanked God for being so lucky in finding each other. They vowed that come what may, they would find some way out to live life king-size, together. They were satiated with each other and vowed never to lose trust in each other. He explored her senses and she explored his weaknesses. Then they reached for the zenith — for the umpteenth time forgetting to take any precaution, throwing caution into the wind.

Then they lay in each other's arms and giggled about how they should get married if she got pregnant.

As if they knew what was going to happen!

CHAPTER 22

September 1994

Durga puja was one-and-a-half months away and their household was getting busier. The larger-than-life-size goddess was being sculpted in their *thakurdalan*. Usually the goddesses were sculpted at a specialized location known as Kumartuli, by professional people. But in the Roy family, the goddess was made by one particular sculptor, who worked with the family since he was a teenager.

Silt from the River Ganges was brought in and stored on the *thakurdalan* in heaps. Then straws and bamboos were brought for the structure of the model. Samir Pal worked in the *thakurdalan* from early morning till midnight. He ate and slept in a room at the ground floor. All the ground floor rooms were opened a month before the festival and got teeming with their relatives from outside Calcutta, who stayed in the house, contributed to the puja financially and helped in the preparations. The kitchen got extremely busy and two new servants were engaged. All guests were treated royally and Digambar Roy kept no stone unturned to see that his visitors were happy.

Tuli got suddenly very responsible and busy. She was suddenly taking her chores seriously and actively participating like a real *bouma* of the household in entertaining the guests. Mahamaya watched her happily. "She's just a kid. She took her obvious time to settle down. I was overreacting." The other two women gossiped furiously. "She's changed so much, did you see?"

"Yes, she's practically becoming the centre of attraction."

"That's okay. She's a new bride. They haven't really spent time with her."

Tuli stayed away from Neil consciously. She had missed her periods and knew that Neil's existence was stirring inside her. Her seriousness grew from that day, ever since she knew that. It was as though she was holding Neil's wealth in her womb. She stopped sliding down the stairs, climbing the tree or smoking cigarettes stolen from her husband's pack during the afternoons in her closed room. She climbed down from the high bed slowly and *walked* down the stairs. She dressed every day, wearing her ornaments and the best of her *saris*. Became regular about her diet and drank lots of water.

Even Soumen noticed the change. How dignified and elegant his wife had become. He was proud of her. But she never let him touch her at night. He missed sex with her. But he never minded. He was visiting a woman after office, anyway. He needed variations.

He never decoded what she was preparing the stage for!

Neil was in a placid state of emotions. He spent a conscious time away from home at his University, trying to figure out what to do about his career. He noticed Tuli becoming increasingly detached from him and getting attached to the family. He felt a weird sense of insecurity and jealousy. He told himself that he was happy. If not anything else, this was a sure positive note for the harmony of the family.

He paced in his room one afternoon. Tuli was not going to college of late as guests were becoming her prime concern. He had stuffed hash in his cigarette and was puffing at it. The smoke clogged his lungs and lifted him off the ground. He felt good. He lay down on his pillow and began thinking categorically.

Where did he stand? What did he want? What did he want to do with his life?

Okay. So he was bothered Tuli was not coming up at all. He was bothered Tuli was getting too close to Soumen. They were even going out for movies together. Normal. Absolutely normal relationship, the way he had wanted. So why was he feeling this insecurity now? What did he feel for her? Love? Can he love his sister-in-law so self-assuredly? Okay. So this was love. What next? He spoke to himself, now what?

Tuli was frantic about Neil. Loved him enormously. And knowing his brother, Neil knew that she was speaking sense about Soumen, about the whole affair.

He felt the airy sensation again and held his head. Then he took another deep puff, wanting to drown himself in a realm of senselessness. He didn't want to think. There was nothing for him to think. He couldn't hurt his family for his own needs.

He closed his eyes. He saw Tuli's face hanging above him. He opened his eyes with a jerk. She was nowhere. He felt his eyes close again and again he saw Tuli. He held out his hand to reach her, but it was too heavy...

CHAPTER 23

Mahalaya, September 22, 1994

On the dawn of *Mahalaya,* Tuli came up to Neil's room for the first time in a month.

White clouds sailed across azure skies with the sun glittering at an angle over golden leaves, making them shimmer in the light cool breeze. *Kaash* flowers, white and aesthetic, burst to bloom, swaying faintly in the zephyr. Bengal burst forth in glory, as if there was never any discontent, any animosity, any acrimony among its men. All ailments were forgotten, all problems got postponed. Even the poorest of the clan bought new clothes and matching accessories. Happiness, harmony and hope looked like they were the only emotions that ruled their convictions. Autumn arrived with its magic, setting the stage for the greatest festival.

For Neil this change was of no auspicious concern. It occurred every year and he was not perturbed. He restricted his movements from his room to the university and back. He met the family at dinner and barely conversed with anyone or looked at Tuli. That was the most tormenting part as he saw Tuli getting closer and closer to Soumen each day. He felt a weird sense of betrayal. He felt insecure. He hated himself for being so vulnerable about his own feelings.

He slept on the eve of *Mahalaya* the way he would do on any other night when he heard the knock.

A soft knock. He woke up startled thinking he was dreaming. And then he heard the knock again.

He stood up slightly wobbly from deep sleep and pulled down the latch. It was dark still. He opened the door. Tuli stood in a nightdress, smiling.

"Good morning!" she smiled.

Neil felt an initial emotion of ecstasy on seeing her. Then he felt irked at his own unshielded emotion.

"What d'you want?" he said groggily, impolitely.

"Won't you listen to *Mahalaya*?" her smile had vanished. But she was still cheerful.

Neil waddled back to the bed. "Oh, God!" he said and threw himself onto the bed. He couldn't deny the happiness inside him, soaring above all anger, on seeing her after a month. He closed his eyes and felt Tuli's fingers run through his hair.

"I know you are angry… and jealous," he heard her say. "And you must be wondering why I have become so serious, so sane. I'll let you know one day… not now…" She stopped. He wondered what she was speaking about. She spoke like a matured adult. He lost his trail of thoughts in an instant dream. Then he heard her again. "Now wake up. See I've even got a transistor." And she switched on the machine. The devotional surge filled the air.

He opened his eyes and tried to wake up. The hymns were dreamlike, permeating inside him to awaken him. For the first time in the twenty-two years of his life, he found he was listening to the lyrics of the Sanskrit chants and trying to comprehend their meaning. He turned on his back and cocked his head to look at Tuli. The room was dark baring the dim bulb burning outside his room. At the reflected hue he could see she was somber and preoccupied with something. She looked out of the window into the darkness that was now slowly blending into dawn.

He wanted to freeze the picture into a frame of eternity and told himself, *"This is the happiest moment of my life."* As if she heard him saying that, and turned to smile at him. His face was parched, but he smiled back.

"You've become quite a *bouma*, huh? Responsible and all that?"

She smiled and looked away. Neil said, "Everyone's raving about you."

She cast her eyes down. "You only asked me to stay away from you. And when I did that, you went mad? Jealous?" She looked at him.

He looked at her for a moment and said, "I wanted it, and you did it?"

"Of course."

He turned to his side and wound his hands around her waist.

"*Dada* isn't awake?"

She shook her head.

"Won't he listen to *Mahalaya*?"

She looked at him and ran her fingers through his hair, "What do you think? Will he?"

Neil buried his face in her lap and said groggily. "And I was happily sleeping thinking that at last you were gone and I was a free man — and you had to wake me up."

The songs and hymns were reaching the climax. The intensity of the emotion wrenched out from the electronic device into their souls and they found themselves silent. As if a voyage was underway; they held their hands and moved towards a haloed resplendence, an existence with no dimension, guided by the devotional inundation as the only witness.

A crow cawed hesitantly, breaking the spell. Another. And then another. Neil looked up and then sat up. He suddenly didn't want to let go of this moment. He wound one hand around her neck and with the other — he cupped her face and made her look at him. She looked at him, a little questioningly. He tilted his head and kissed her lightly on her lips. Then he smiled and said very softly, *"Let's run away…"!!*

She broke into a smile and hugged him. The next instant she went stiff and released him slowly. He looked at her bewildered. Her face was a horror as she looked at the doorway. He jerked his head around.

Soumen was standing at the door!…

REMO

CHAPTER 1

Mumbai, January 27, 1995

For Remo, traveling in Mumbai never posed a threat. While his contemporaries sweated in clamorous local trains running chaotically across the city, he was provided with one exclusive vehicle after another. Ever since he took on Hassan, he was showered with the best accessories of life. Remo himself was smart and took on '*supari*'s [30] within a year of migrating into the wonder city.

Here how money flew like the waters of a tide and fell into the laps of those who chose to understand and recognize it! Who said India is a poor land, specializing in poverty and disillusion? Who said India can't beat the world in wealth? One had just to walk into the homes of the kinds as Hassan and laugh at such weird notions.

His Ibrahim *bhai* was shooting into power every day. He technically ruled a section of the city. Ministers, actors from films, police commissioners and other city dons from all over the city acclaimed his supremacy alike. However, Ibrahim Hassan himself was an unassuming man. An honest man. He was honest about the distribution of his booty among his men. He was honest about sending money home — in a remote village in the state of Bihar, where his wife stayed with two grown-up sons, who engaged themselves in tilling their land. He never betrayed anyone or forgot a betrayal. He had immigrated into the city years back in search of an existence and found one, not very suited to his principles, but very suited to his imaginations. He rose from the shambles by sheer 'honesty'. He was proud of his integrity.

Remo Gujjar was the most coveted man in the 55-year-old king's dynasty. "The 26-year-old boy is a marvel," Ibrahim had often thought. "He'll take on my empire once I am gone." He stored a part of his wealth for Gina, his very loyal mistress who catered to his needs so that he never missed his wife. A barrage of women lined up for his nights and he gave each one a chance. Gina knew about that and never minded as long as she got her part of the distribution. She too led her life and catered to the needs of the prime men in Hassan's kingdom. Everyone needed everybody and there was no jealousy among his men.

Remo leant over his balcony above twelve floors. This sprawling flat bang on Juhu Beach was a present from Hassan after he had done away with one of his stark enemies. He wiped his Ray-Ban sunglasses on his Calvin Klein T-shirt and stuck them into his Lee jeans. Two years back he would never have dreamt of possessing those designer names. He hadn't heard of them, was innocent and naive when he had moved into Mumbai from the slums of Calcutta looking for a job. His distant uncle had a large house in Pali Hill and he had thought, like his father had, that this well-settled businessman cousin of his father could well put him up in a job.

Reality dawned on him after a month that he was appointed as an unpaid servant in their house. He was barely 24, but had a sharp mind. The daughter of his uncle was a kind woman, who stayed with her father after having been deserted by her husband. She taught him a lot in that single month, including sex. It was she who helped him run away and got him introduced to one of Hassan's men. The big man liked him instantly and the rest became history.

"You take on Juhi," Remo announced and looked at Neil, who was sitting in one of the cane chairs in the balcony and clipping his nails with a cutter. Neil looked up, shocked.

"You're mad?"

"I've paid her advance. Now she'll charge the entire amount."

The sky was getting overcast again. The untimely shower spell a while ago made the sea in front of them raging. The wild winds swung the flowerpots hanging from the ceiling of the balcony. It was technically winter and the air had gotten chillier than before but the interrupting sea breeze warmed the atmosphere. It was never too cold in Mumbai.

It was almost six in the evening and Juhi, who was to accompany Remo for that night's party had not arrived yet.

"Why don't you wait?" Neil said.

"No. I have to report to *Bhai* at seven. I can't afford to be late."

Neil looked down and began clipping his toenails.

"Where would I take her? Why would she want to go with me?"

Remo said cheekily, "That's your problem, honey. Here're three more thousand bucks. Give it to her after you've finished." He handed the thin bunch of 500 rupee notes and strode out of the balcony. He looked over his shoulders after opening the door and teased, "Don't soil my bedspread, okay?" Then he banged the door shut and was gone.

Neil finished clipping his nails and stood up for a shower. He kept the money on the glass and brass center table in the sitting room and took his clothes out from his closet. Jeans and a yellow T-shirt. Not blue. *That had been bloodstained!*

It was almost seven and the daylight was almost fading. Mumbai is, incidentally, located at the western extreme of India and had one of the longest days in the entire country. He showered, dressed and walked out in the balcony. It was a Sunday and the beach was teeming with people. The sun had set into the sea a while ago and the sky looked a cataclysmic kaleidoscope of orange, blue and red. Marine Drive was already sparkling with ignited streetlights. The entire city lit up — as if it was waiting for the sky to turn dark — when the fervent giant called nightlife in Mumbai could wake up!

There was nothing more to see. There wasn't much to do either after sundown if you didn't have the right circle of acquaintances. Here in Mumbai, finding friends is tough. There were mostly business deals. If you had nothing tangible to offer anyone, not many wanted you. Neil knew that. He had an interview for a sales job the next day. He was not interested in Remo's lifestyle.

He walked back and switched on the lights. He inserted a Hindi remix cassette from Remo's shelf into the Sony music deck. There was nothing else to do but wait for this call girl. For dinner he would go to a nearby *dhaba* [31].

He had to get a job.

The bell rang. Must be the girl. He didn't know how to react to this girl. He opened the door.

She was standing in a black long skirt and a colorful pullover. A purse was slung over her shoulders and she wore high platform heels. Her hair was straight up to her shoulders and she wore garish make-up and a strong perfume.

"Can I talk to Remo?"

Neil opened the door wide. "I'm sorry... he had to leave. He waited for a long time for you. You're Juhi, right?"

"Yes," she half smiled, half angry.

"Hi!" Neil extended his hand, "I'm Neil. Come in."

"Hi!" She walked in.

He closed the door.

"Please sit down." He lowered the volume of the music.

Juhi hesitated. And then finding no other option, sat down.

"You mean... he left?"

Neil sat opposite her. "Er... he was getting late."

"Come on," Juhi was angry. "You can't call a girl and then simply dump her."

Neil smiled. He didn't know whom to stand up for, Remo or her. He didn't know who was wrong. This city had rules he couldn't fathom during his stay here for the past two months.

"I'm sorry, I'm sure you can... er... find yourself at home here. Can I be of any help?"

She looked away disgusted. "Can I have something to drink?"

"Oh sure!" Neil leapt up. Then stopped. "What would you like?"

"Dry gin. With soda."

"Okay." Neil nodded and opened the drinks' cabinet. A barrage of bottles greeted him. He read the labels. Old Monk Rum, Bacardi, Seagram's whiskey. Dry gin… dry gin… yes! There was Blue Ribbon. Extra dry gin. He took out the bottle and poured a peg into a tumbler. Then he took out the soda from the fridge and mixed it with the colorless liquid.

"Ice?" he asked.

"Yes please."

He dug out the ice tray from the freezer and dropped two cubes into the frothy liquid.

"Here," he handed her the liquid. "You'll feel nice."

Juhi smiled at the sight of it and took the glass. She was a shade cooler.

She sipped on the liquid and crossed her legs. "Won't you like one?"

"Er… yes. Just a minute." He walked to the cabinet and looked at the bottles. What would he like? Let's try Bacardi white Rum this time. He poured himself a peg and added cold water. He had started getting familiar with this lifestyle only after an initial rebuff. It was a necessity in Mumbai to know and mix drinks. Also to taste all the liquids and not get drunk.

He sat opposite her with his drink and smiled. Juhi smiled back. He looked around for a conversation. What do you converse with a call girl? Why was she doing all this? That was the foremost question in his mind. He ruled it out categorically. Perhaps, he should start with where she stayed, or who all were there in her family. Considering the conservative family he hailed from, it was difficult for him to begin a conversation without knowing a little of the person's background.

He ruled out all of it and decided to talk about the weather.

"You've been here in Mumbai for long?"

Juhi looked up. He prayed it was not a wrong question.

"For four years now." She calculated.

Now it became more complicated. Where was she *before* this?

He tried framing another question, when *she* spoke. "You are Remo's friend? I've never seen you before."

"No that's because I am here only for two months." Neil let out a silent sigh as Juhi took charge of the conversation.

"No wonder! I had been out of station." She looked at him from the corner of her eye. "You plan to join Hassan?"

"Join Hassan? No. I'm Remo's friend. I've come here looking for a job." He became slightly defensive.

"Job?" she crooned. "What kind of job are you looking for?" Juhi ran her forefingers on the tumbler, drawing lines on the condensed droplets of water. Neil looked at her questioningly. She looked as though she had quite a few vacancies in her pocket.

"A job in sales, perhaps."

"You have computer knowledge?" Juhi sounded professional.

"A little."

"Hmm…" she looked down and nodded. As if trying to decide which job to assign him to.

He burst into a smile, "You have some ready at hand?"

She looked up, a little displeased. "If you want, I can speak to some people," she shrugged.

Neil leant back, "I don't have much choice, do I?"

"Okay," she took out a visiting card from her purse. "Give me a ring here tomorrow at three. I'll see what I can do."

Juhi gulped down the rest of the liquid and stood up.

"You're leaving?" Neil asked sincerely.

"Yah, what else would I do?"

Neil decided to get over with the dirty job. "Er… Remo gave me some money he owes you." He took out the notes from his pocket and extended the wad hesitantly to her.

She looked at them, "Owes me? He doesn't owe me any money."

A faint rebuke supported a confident voice with which he next spoke.

"Three thousand bucks that he was supposed to give you tonight."

Juhi looked at him as though she was about to slap him. Then she bit out every word. "I am not *that* hard up for money." And turned and slammed the door behind her.

Neil heaved a sigh. He walked over and finished his drink. Then took the two glasses and washed them. Then he walked out to the balcony. He looked down and saw a green Maruti speeding off from the car park.

He lit a cigarette and plopped down on the cane chair.

Through the ornate railings he could see the phosphorous-smeared sea calmer and softer. The sky had a red hue. Clouds had not left the territory. The stars were all hidden. An airplane roared low beneath the red sky with alternate red and yellow lights flickering on it. It was going eastward. Perhaps towards Calcutta.

He sighed and leant back. *He was far away from home.*

Home. He touched his forehead. Yes, it still hurt. The stitch mark was prominent. A bitter taste filled his soul. He didn't want to remember...

CHAPTER 2

Calcutta, September 22, 1994

Soumen saw them kissing and hugging and stormed out of the room. Neil and Tuli looked at each other, petrified. Then Neil reacted.

He ran after his brother.

"*Dada*!" he called out.

Soumen stopped and turned. He had a dangerous look in his eyes. Neil walked up to him. He didn't know what he would say. But he had to face it one day. This was the time.

The terrace was getting brighter with daylight and despite the innocence that the dawn spewed around, Soumen's eyes were screaming with hatred.

"*Dada*, I wanted to speak to you about this for a long time… Tuli and I …"

"Shut up! You bastard!"

"*Dada*, please, can't we sit down and speak?"

Soumen moved towards Neil and let his hands fly. It rung right across Neil's face so powerfully that he fell right on his back.

Tuli watched in horror and came running when she saw this.

"Soumen, please." Her voice was composed despite the fear. "Please listen to what Neil has to say."

In reply Soumen walked over and pounced on Tuli's arm, trying to pull her off to go down with him. Tuli wrenched her hand free.

"You don't possess me. I am not your slave." She let out.

Soumen looked shocked. "You bitch…! Come with me! I'll fix you." He tried to hold her hand again. She moved away. Neil stood up and tried to calm his brother. He held him and tried to speak.

"Listen, we can work out something with sanity. Don't wake up the whole house." In reply Soumen hit him once again across his face. Neil reeled but stood aground. Though thin, he was strong enough to could physically throw Soumen into the courtyard. That would have solved all problems. But he didn't do it. He had his priorities straight.

Tuli came in front of Neil and said, "Soumen, Neil and I are in love with each other. It is nobody's fault. Not even yours. We can work out something…"

"You bitch! How could you?? I am sending you to your home. You don't know my powers."

He threatened them with his fingers and stomped out of the terrace.

Tuli instantly ran into Neil's arms and held him tight — silent tears of apprehension rolling down her cheeks.

Neil patted on her cheek. Then felt the tears.

"Hey? You faced *Kalboishakhi*. You weren't scared then. Why, this storm isn't even a gale."

Tuli looked up to him. Blood was trickling down his lips.

"Oh, my God!" She freed herself and pulled him to the water tap. Turning the cap, she cupped water in her palm and smeared it over his lips. She washed off the blood. He licked his lips and said, "It's okay. I'd been beaten up more severely in school."

"But you do workouts, couldn't you at least defend yourself?"

"No. I wanted him to vent his anger on me. That would cool him."

This time Tuli spoke. "Are you for real? Or do you playact?"

Neil laughed. And pulled her towards him. And held her. And said. "Now let's go down and face the raging world. Let's see how we tackle it, okay?"

Tuli nodded. *For the first time in her life she was scared!*

The house was asleep. The faint rhythm of the conclusion of Mahalaya still rung through the sleepy rooms. Light was burning in

Mahamaya's room. Neil held Tuli's hand and knocked on the door. Then pushed it open. Soumen and Mahamaya sat on the bed. Their facial expression said that Soumen had already related the horror-tale to his mother. Neil closed the door.

"Ma," he said. "Are you willing to speak to me?"

"What is there to speak?" Mahamaya looked disgustedly at Tuli.

Suddenly the elderly lady came charging at Tuli, "This girl is the ill-omened thing in this house." And raised her hand for a slap. This time Neil pounced on her and held her hand.

"No physical demonstrations in this house." He led her back and continued holding her hand and said, "I am responsible for all this. Ma please, why don't we speak like mature people?"

"Mature?" Soumen spoke, "She behaves like a *randi* [32] and you expect to speak…"

"*Dada!*" Neil raised his voice. He turned to Tuli and said softly, "Sorry…" The object of the storm stood expressionless. Her eyes dry. In reality she felt the whole thing was happening to somebody else. Happening in her nightmare. She wanted to sit down. She felt the world closing in on her. Her ears were ringing and her was mouth feeling dry…

Neil held his patience, "*Dada*, Ma, the whole thing is nobody's fault…"

"It was her fault!" Tuli heard her mother-in-law say. She closed her eyes. Her whole world was swaying.

"No," Neil was speaking. "She was neglected and not understood by any of you. Did you try to understand her, *Dada*? Pardon me for saying; you were interested in her only physically. Did you ever try to see what she wanted emotionally? Her emotions? Her feelings? Her madness? Did you try to look beyond her figure?"

"Neilu!" snapped Mahamaya. "That is not your territory. You cannot speak like that to your elder brother."

"Why not? This was the reason behind her attachment to me. What's wrong if I try to explain…"

He trailed off. Tuli had fallen on the ground. *She had fainted!*

CHAPTER 3

The doctor came out of the room and all three of them, Soumen, Mahamaya and Doctor Bhattacharya beamed. Neil stood motionless leaning on a pillar in the balcony. The sun was up, but the household lay in bed on a holiday mood. Manik was the only busybody around.

Neil didn't know why they were smiling. He was tempted to ask. But Soumen had taken complete charge of his wife after she had fainted. Picking her up, putting her on the bed and running for water. Then he took out the car and fetched the gynecologist. Everything. Even Mahamaya didn't let Neil come anywhere near Tuli. She kept asking him to go back to sleep. He couldn't. He remembered the prediction and feared the worst.

However, he was perplexed at seeing their beaming faces. If not anything, it meant all was well.

They went past him and Soumen ignored him completely.

Neil walked forward. "Ma how's she?"

"She's fine." Mahamaya cut in. "Why don't you go back to sleep?"

Neil nodded, peeped into Soumen's room. He couldn't see her. He walked back upstairs.

He lit a smoke. The world was collapsing around him. But he tried to be positive and tell himself that whatever was happening was for good.

CHAPTER 4

September 26, 1994

Neil refused to see Tuli after that day. Something at the back of his mind told him he'd lost.

He went out for jogs early in the morning, ate outside mostly. Then he delved himself completely into his university life. Rather self-destructively. Indulging in hashish and heroin —which became his full-time occupation. He was slowly becoming an addict and he liked it.

The goddess Durga was now fully sculpted on their *thakurdalan*. Gleaming ornaments and amber attire made her look mystical and omnipotent. He stood near the *thakurdalan* a day before the *pujas* and prayed. For the first time in his life. He prayed for Tuli. For himself. It was afternoon and the courtyard was empty. He folded his hands and closed his eyes. Then he raised his hands on his forehead and brought it down. He opened his eyes.

Tuli was standing upstairs, leaning her head onto the railings of the balcony, watching him. She had a pacified smile on her face. And on seeing he was looking at her, raised her eyebrows as if to say, "Hi! What's up?"

Neil knew that gesture. She could crumble inside but make others feel wonderful. He smiled. But tears stung his eyes. He got the message. He had not lost.

He ran upstairs quickly, fearing he'd encounter her again. He didn't.

It was after four days that he had to take a decision.

CHAPTER 5

Mahasthami, September 30, 1994

Mahasthami. The climactic day of the festival. The entire household had been downstairs since dawn in new clothes and ornaments. The women wore a red liquid, called *alta*, on their feet, and *anchal* over their heads. The men wore *dhoti* [33] and silk *kurtas* [34]. Everything smelt of flowers, incense and happiness. The *dhaki* (drummer) played on the drum incessantly. The goddess was obliterated in a thick smoke from the incense.

Neil was feeling nauseated. He was woken up at five in the morning by the sound of the drums. He stuck around in his room till late morning. He asked Manik to serve him tea and breakfast in his room. Mahamaya came up once wearing a red-bordered crème-colored sari and lots of jewelry. She said, "At least, come down today. Put on your new clothes and come down. Everyone's missing you."

He shook his head in negative. "I have work to do. I have to go out."

Mahamaya didn't say a thing. She didn't know how long it'd take for things to revert to normalcy. Whether it would at all, or not. She didn't know what she should do about the whole affair.

Neil went out around lunchtime wearing Tuli's favorite blue T-shirt and jeans. He, rather, crept out in the midst of a dramatic *aaroti* [35] being performed in the *thakurdalan,* that transformed the arena into some kind of a transcending mystery.

He subconsciously scanned the crowd. And then he spotted her. She was standing on the *thakurdalan* and had seen him. Her eyes said, "Don't go."

He lowered his eyes, heaved a sigh and crept out. The streets were dusty and sunny. It was a warm day.

"Neil…" He turned around. Tuli had come out with all the ornaments, a peacock blue *kanjivaram* sari with the *aanchal* over her head. Her feet were bare!

She came running to him. He stood transfixed. She had never looked so beautiful before!

"Where are you going?" she panted.

"Go back! You shouldn't come out like this." He scanned around. People were beginning to notice her.

"Don't go anywhere. Please stay back." She was pleading, her eyes watery.

"Why?" Neil asked before he realized it.

"Because I love you. Because I am dying inside… Because I can't stay a moment without you… and I am doing so for a month."

He lowered his eyes. "Go back inside. I'll come back fast." He smiled and extended his hand to usher her inside. He hesitated. She looked like a delicate possession. Something unobtainable.

"Tuli!" Soumen came out of the house, instantly. Tuli swung her head around and stood defiant. "Come back inside!"

"Go," Neil said softly.

She looked at Neil with eyes that said so many things. Then turned back and ran inside.

Neil resumed his steps.

Once inside Soumen held her arm with a fierceness that could crumble her bones.

"I warned you…" he bit the words. But kept a faint smile on for outsiders. She stood numb. Let her hand crumble…let her entire existence crumble… *No!* No. She had Neil inside her!

She slowly released her hand and went upstairs. She entered her room and closed out the noise. She was alone.

She picked up her sari from her belly and protruded it towards the mirror.

"So? Hi-ah shweetheart? How's it inside?"

Soumen had followed her. Then seeing that she was inside, crossed his own room and entered Mahamaya's. *He picked up the telephone receiver and dialed...*

CHAPTER 6

Mahasthami **evening**

Remo Gujjar was in Mumbai, but his flat that he had bought in Alipore, a posh area of Calcutta, recently, after had he started working in Mumbai, was used by two of his friends, Ambik and Harris. Ambik was from Konnagar, a town outside Calcutta, couldn't find accommodation in his college hostel and Harris had difficulty staying with his parents in Lee Road, south of Calcutta. They both paid rent to Remo who visited the city every month-end for all his collections.

Remo had bought a smaller flat for his parents in South Calcutta. The flat was, maybe cheaper, but located in the most convenient place in Calcutta, Lake Road, near the lakes. Remo's father had spent his entire life in the slums and this two-bed roomed, south-facing dream was something he blessed his son for.

Remo's flat in Alipore was something his parents didn't know about. His father knew nothing about Remo's job. But he and Remo's mother were happy. Their last days were nearing. What more could they want?

Neil found this den through his journey through drugs. He had met Remo a couple of times. He didn't find anything to like or hate about him. Ambik and Harris were sunk throat-deep in their addiction in smack.

They hated to go out during the *pujas* and watched cable TV instead, when Neil rang their doorbell.

"Hi!" opened Harris. "You're here? Isn't there a celebration in your house?"

"Yah," added Ambik plopped on a mattress on the ground, which served both as a sofa and a bed. The 14" color TV was bought by both of them in installments. "We were planning to drop in towards the evening. We were getting bored."

Neil smiled dryly. He was in no mood for a conversation. He walked over to the kitchen and dipped a glass in a bucket of water. He drank it. He was thirsty. Alipore was in an inconvenient location. One had to possess a car, and then all became easy. He had had to walk a long way.

"What's the matter? You're so quiet? Want a joint?" asked Ambik. He hadn't gone back home for the *pujas*. His middle-class parents in Konnagar were under the impression that their son was immersed in studying Economics.

Neil nodded. He plopped down beside them on the mattress and stuffed a pillow behind him. Rushes of new films were being showed on the TV. He watched it disinterestedly. Harris walked over to the kitchen and took a packet from the top of the shelf.

Ambik began emptying out a cigarette on that day's newspaper.

"It's becoming costlier," said Harris as he handed the packet of marijuana to him. "Chhotu was grumbling that day."

"How much?" asked Neil. He had a fat wallet. His dad had just given him his pocket money.

"Forty."

"That's okay," Neil clicked his tongue and reached out to give a hand to Ambik in making the joint.

They mixed a part of the contents of the packet with the tobacco. And then, carefully stuffed the product back into the cigarette.

"Hey, we can have that leftover Bacardi," Harris suddenly remembered.

"Oh great, where's it?" said Neil.

"Under the table in the kitchen."

"I'll make it." Neil got up. The bottle was half-empty. "Who got the bottle?" Neil came out with three glasses and the bottle.

"*Aarre*, Remo was here day-before," said Ambik. "We had two-and-a-half bottles the whole night. Couldn't finish the third."

"Remo was here? He didn't call me?" Neil asked.

"No, he's very busy. He's bought a sprawling flat in Juhu," said Harris.

"I think Hassan gave't to him," quipped Ambik.

"Who cares?" said Neil as he poured the drinks. Ambik passed on the prepared joint. Neil lit his very carefully, pulling on the smoke hard. He passed it on to Ambik.

"Who's going to get the water, you skunk?" Harris said as he got up to get a bottle of water from the kitchen.

The marijuana felt good. Harris mixed water with the rum and passed the glasses to his friends. They raised the glasses. "Cheers!"

"Let's celebrate *Ashtami!*" said Ambik.

Harris laughed.

Neil didn't feel like laughing.

He took the joint and pulled hard at the smoke instead. He gulped down the smoke and held it in his lungs. Then released it part-by-part into the air.

Their world began swaying soon. Neil wanted to sleep. He had been awake for a long time. He lay down on a pillow. He was never too fond of drinking. His glass remained half-finished. But he was fast asleep already.

....Tuli was running down the stairs... her hair loose... she was screaming something... she was very scared... She tried to reach Neil... but she couldn't... She was being pulled into a blackness behind her. Neil couldn't reach out. His feet were sunk into the ground... he held out his hands and called out her name... Tuli...Tuli...

"TULI..." He woke up shaking. It was dark. Oh, what a nightmare! He touched his head. Perspiration. He tried to see through the darkness. Where was everybody? What time was it? Even the TV was switched off.

He slowly stood up and fumbled in the darkness for the light switch. He felt the wall and felt for the button. He found the switchboard. He didn't know which switch was for the light. He lit the first one. And then the second. Light filled the room.

No one was there! Barring the empty glasses and cigarette butts strewn haywire, the room was empty. Almost eerie! He looked at his watch. 11:15 p.m.!

God! Did he sleep that long? Everyone must be paranoid back home. Tuli! She must be frantic!

He waddled towards the door. The grass was still lifting him off-ground. Bacardi was a strong mix. He reached for the handle. Did they lock him and go?

He turned the handle. It opened.

He closed the door behind him and raced down the stairs. The road outside was deserted and ghostly. This part of the city was a sophisticated, non-Bengali zone. Nobody celebrated the festival here. There were no lights, no drums, no happy faces around. The roads were dark and eerie like any other road at midnight.

His feet raced. He had to catch a bus. Would he get any at this hour? Maybe he should take an auto-rickshaw to Hazra. Maybe he'll get a bus from there.

The roads were empty. No such luck. He began walking towards Hazra crossing. It was a long walk and his feet felt heavy. He looked around for a taxi. He had to get home fast. He had promised her, he'd be back soon.

One empty taxi rolled in from the opposite side.

"Taxi!" he called out.

The driver looked out. "Where?"

"Bowbazar."

The driver nodded his head and zoomed off.

He had to walk. The unpredictable taxi-drivers' moods were the last thing he wanted to encounter.

In almost half-an-hour he reached Hazra. Here bright lights welcomed him. The streets were crowded, as though it was evening. Happy faces walked about, touring through the *pandals*. Cars, honks, songs over loudspeaker and squealing kids with balloons in their hands woke him up to reality. He felt better.

Another taxi! He waddled towards it.

"Bowbazar. I'll pay you extra."

The driver nodded and pulled down the meter. The four-wheeler took off.

Puja was getting more and more conspicuous in this part of the city. Strings of lights hung down from buildings. And flickering lights lined up the footpaths. Teeming crowd jostled past heavy traffic. Neil couldn't do much but plop on the seat and wait for the vehicle to move.

He reached Bowbazar at 12:35 a.m. This part of the city too teemed with excitement. He felt, maybe his folks wouldn't be so worried after all.

He parked the cab outside the narrow lane that led into his house. He paid the driver and got off.

The lane was darker and less gay. His house was lit, however. The light was on in Ma's room. She was awake. He walked a few more steps. Light was on in *her* room. *She* must be awake too! He quickened his steps. *He couldn't live without her... He loved her too much... He had to take a decision... He...*

"Aaahhh...!!"

Somebody hit the side of his head with a hard object. He fell down. A series of kicks. And punches. On his stomach and back. He coiled up his knees and tried opening his eyes. He couldn't. Somebody's shoes hit his nose. He heard a crack. It must be broken. He turned to face them and raised his hands to defend himself. Another blow. This time with the same hard object on his stomach. He cringed with pain. He was going to die. *Somebody was killing him.* He heard male voices shouting and feet scampering off...

CHAPTER 7

Neil opened his eyes in an alien room. He felt numb and stared at the reeling fan. He tried to turn his head. It felt stiff. He tried to lift his right hand. It was attached to a small tube full of blood, which led to a bottle full of the same liquid. Another bottle with colorless liquid hung above him. He lifted his left hand and touched his forehead. His face was bandaged, so was his forehead. He ran a palm over his face. Baring his eyes, lips and nostrils, everything was bandaged. He tried sitting up.

"No, no," said an alien female voice from behind. "You can't get up."

The voice took form. She came in front. She was a nurse and smiled at him. "Wait till your mother hears you are awake."

"Whe…" No sound came out. He cleared his throat. "Where am I?"

"At Presidency Nursing Home."

"How many days …?"

"Three days. Now don't talk so much or you'll start bleeding again. I'll call your mother."

He closed his eyes. He was attacked and beaten up by some ruffians. Why? What did they want? Did they take anything? His money? Why didn't they ask for it? Why did they beat him up?

"Neilu…" He opened his eyes and looked at his mother. Like a child, a baby — he didn't remember when she had last taken him in her lap, when she hugged her fears away — he cried. Soft tears flooded down his temples, wetting the bandage.

Mahamaya held his hand and then hugged him. She loved him so much. But she was afraid of Soumen's increasing powers.

They both cried.

"Where's Tuli?" Neil finally said.

Instantly her mother's embrace became stiff. She pulled up. Tears were running down her eyes, but her face had become steel.

"Neilu," she tried to explain, "She's your sister-in-law. How could you...?"

He turned away. His tears stopped midway. He suddenly didn't feel like explaining her anything.

"Forget her. See what happened to you?"

He was perplexed. "What do you mean?"

"Nothing." She cast her eyes down.

"No more talking," the nurse announced.

"What is it, Ma?"

"Nothing. Now go back to sleep. We'll come again tomorrow."

She left, after holding his hand.

Neil felt his eyes becoming heavy. What did she mean ? Could *Dada* have...?

No. *Dada* wouldn't do such a thing. No way! His mind went blank as he fell into a sedative sleep.

He woke up again the next day. He saw Tuli. He felt he was dreaming and opened his eyes wide.

"Hi!" she said, smiling.

"Wha...? How did you...?" He tried to sit up. Tuli held his hand.

"Lie down, my sweetheart. You are looking like a picture." She laughed, "A cartoon picture."

"How did you come?"

"I came." She smiled and pulled a stool to sit beside him. "See I brought flowers for you." She handed him a bunch of red roses. He lifted his left hand and took them. "They're beautiful. What's the time?"

"It's nine in the morning."

"It's not visiting hours yet."

"Yah, that's why I could come. I came out of the house to go to college."

"And how did you get in here?"

"I convinced people around. They are quite nice, you know. I told them that I was your sister-in-law and would leave the city in an hour, so I had to see you."

He laughed. "You're incorrigible!"

She took the flowers from his hands and placed them in a vase on his bedside table.

Then she turned to him. She was very serious.

"Remember, you had a friend in Mumbai?"

"Yah, Remo. Why?"

"Why don't you spend a few days with him?"

Neil stared at her. She lowered her eyes. "I want you to go."

He watched her for a few moments. "You really want me to go?"

She looked at him and pressed her lips. "I want to see you happy."

"I am happy."

"With all this bandage?" She smiled.

"No, this was an accident."

She said slowly, "The next time *I* might have an accident."

This time the bell rang. Neil crossed his brows despite the stiff forehead. "What is it, Tuli? What are you trying to say? What are you trying to hide from me?"

"Neil," Tuli held his hand. "You make a career for yourself. Away from me. I'll wait for you to come back. Then it'll be easier for us to think of something."

He nodded his head. "That's a good idea. But what did you mean by saying you'll have an accident?"

Tuli smiled, "Idiot, I was joking."

Neil didn't believe her. She was definitely hiding something from him.

"I won't be able to come again," she explained. "You'll be coming home in a few days. I'll see you then."

She bent and kissed his lips. Then smiled and left the room.

CHAPTER 8

When Neil came back home after a week, Tuli and Soumen were in Katoa. They had gone there to spend a weekend, informed Mahamaya. Manik catered to all his needs. Mahamaya wanted Neil to sleep downstairs so that she could keep a constant watch over him. He refused. He wanted to think straight. He wanted to speak to his father. Things were going out of his hands. He had to take a decision.

Digambar Roy was a little upset at his younger son's lifestyle. But he wasn't the kind to give up hope so soon. He was an unimposing kind of a husband who let the woman of the house take decisions in household matters. He didn't like interfering too much. But, now he felt, he should have been more vigilant, more alert about the way Mahamaya was bringing up her sons. He didn't know anything about Tuli's involvement with Neil. But he sensed something was seriously wrong. He came up to see Neil on the Saturday evening. Work pressure was lesser and he had some time on his hands.

Neil was sitting on the bed, leaning on the wall, reading a book. Most of his bandages had been taken off.

"How are you feeling today?" Digambar pulled a chair beside him.

"Fine." Neil shut the book. His father suddenly felt it had been a long time since he had spoken to his son. He had been so quiet and undemanding. All the conversation they had were through Manik at the onset of each month for Neil's pocket money, which he insisted on giving.

"What happened exactly?" He was concerned.

Neil looked at him, "I don't know. I was walking back home. It was pretty late, past midnight. I was almost home when a bunch of ruffians attacked me."

Digambar lowered his voice. "Are you involved in something? Some kind of a racket?" he asked simply. He knew this much, that if Neil had been involved, he would not hide it.

"No," Neil simply said. "I was coming back from a friend's house."

"Hmm..." senior Roy nodded. "Should I lodge a complaint?"

"You haven't still?"

He shook his head. "No. I wanted to be sure you were innocent."

"Forget it. I don't think you should lodge a complaint. The honor of the family would be at stake." Something at the back of his mind made him say this. He suspected who was behind this.

He nodded his head. He was happy Neil was so considerate.

"I want to talk to you about something," Neil said.

Digambar looked up.

"I am planning to go to Bombay... Mumbai. I have a friend there who wanted me to come over there for a long time. I want to start a career there."

"Bombay? But you have two years of University!"

"That can't be helped. I am becoming a burden on you. I want to stand on my own feet. "

His father looked thoughtful. "That's okay. But... Bombay? It's a place full of swindlers."

Neil sighed. "I need some money to support myself initially before I get a job. Of course, it'll be a loan. I'll return it."

"When do you want to go?"

"As soon as the doctor tells me I'm fine."

"Okay," Digambar stood up. "I'll write a cheque of fifty thousand for you. You can make drafts or traveler's cheques, whatever."

"I don't need that much," Neil looked up.

His father smiled. "You don't have to pay me back. Who do I earn for anyway?"

He smiled and left. Neil felt a piece of reassuring ground creeping in back beneath his feet. He was never going to forget what his father did for him.

CHAPTER 10

Tuli and Soumen came back the next evening. Throughout the trip, which she was forced to take, she had kept up a patient countenance. She barely smiled and was hardly responsive to her cousins' exuberance over their brother-in-law, who seemed to bask in their attention, or to her mother who kept asking her what's wrong. Srimati remembered Mahi*babu*'s prediction and felt scared. Tuli didn't even feel like telling anybody she was pregnant. Not ever her mother. She was not ready for a festival yet. That too a festival where everybody would celebrate thinking it was Soumen's descendant. Luckily, Soumen too didn't mention it.

She stepped inside her in-laws' house and heaved a sigh of relief. Neil was back home. She had to find an opportunity to see him.

The opportunity came not before Monday afternoon. Neil had come down for lunch and for the first time Mahamaya was not around. Tuli knew she was downstairs seeing off the last of the relatives.

They were eating alone.

None of them spoke for a long time, while Manik served the food. Then Neil spoke.

"You didn't go to college?"

Tuli shook his head. "I have a stomach upset." Then looked up and smiled cheekily.

Stomach upset? Look at her eating all this now. "Ma knows?"

She nodded in affirmation.

"She didn't cook boiled vegetables for you?"

She nodded. "I threw them down the drain."

He sighed, "What a price you have to be married in the Roy family!"

Tuli looked at him. His nose was still bandaged. "How's your nose?"

"Cracked…" he cringed it up. "Better."

They ate silently. It was getting slightly dark outside. It might be the rains once again. Thank God, the rains spared the *puja* days.

The looming dining hall with gothic furniture and a single lamp shade set a mysterious ambiance. They finished their food in silence.

"If I really take your advice and go to Bombay…" Neil said and drank water. He was waiting for her reaction.

She looked up. Her black eyes a shade darker. Her face devoid of color.

Neil shrugged, "I didn't want to. You only asked me…"

Tuli nodded and tried to bring back her composure. She looked down. Unable to speak or eat.

Neil leant back, "I cannot lay a goddamn foot in this world without a bank balance. I need one. I am going to have one, whatever the cost maybe."

She looked up and forced a smile. She didn't realize she was mentally moving away from him after Neil's accident. She knew Soumen was behind it. She knew he could do worse. She wanted to set Neil free. She didn't want any kind of obligation to bind him. Not even their child. Of course she'd understand if he wanted to marry someone else… *of course she would…*

Neil looked at her and smiled. Then toyed with the glass. He was mentally moving away from her after the accident. He was sure who was behind the accident. He was scared for Tuli. He wanted to leave her with Soumen. Completely alone. Maybe matters would improve between them when he came back after a few years. He'd obviously accept it… of course he would… He would find a girl for himself… *of course he would…*

They both looked at each other and tried to mask their thoughts with added smiles. They were both hiding a lot of facts from each other. They were scared for each other's safety. They felt moving away from each other was the best for the situation.

They didn't have a clue about what God had in mind!

CHAPTER 11

Mumbai, January 28, 1995

The interview was a 'set up' one. Neil could make out from the disinterested panel of judges. He came out of the office feeling hungry. He didn't feel like going back home. Remo wouldn't be there anyway. He took an auto-rickshaw to Bandra Beach.

The sea seemed the only warm characteristic of this city to Neil. The sun was cocked at an angle, high up. It was cooler today and the sun-rays felt good. He felt like taking a dip in the waters. But he wasn't Tuli. He smiled at the last thought. Tuli wouldn't have been bothered. She would have run wild in the waters.

He sat down on a comfortable stretch of sand. The beach was nearly empty and stray slum children played on it. Not many people came here on a warm sunny noon. Least of all, in starched interview clothes.

A coconut seller was approaching him. He felt the man read his thoughts. He was just beginning to feel thirsty. He took the fruit and paid the man. He finished the juice in a few gulps. Then he looked for a comfortable spot and laid his head on his files and stretched, making himself feel unperturbed by anybody around. What he didn't realize was that he was adopting Tuli's attitude to life. And it was a difficult task. The sun was warm and he felt his eyes close.

He woke up at around two-thirty. Then shook off the sand from his trousers and began taking strides towards Bandstand. He was thinking of Juhi. He had to make a call at three.

CHAPTER 12

Mumbai, February 19, 1995

The air was getting nippy. The sky was getting overcast and hiding the sun. It was the untimely rains again, perhaps. It was almost four o'clock in the evening. Remo wouldn't be back till the next day.

Neil came back into the bedroom from the balcony and stubbed his cigarette in an ashtray. Juhi was awake. The covers slipped off her bare shoulders as she extended her fingers. "Light me one."

Neil lit her a cigarette. She sat up and pulled the covers over her breasts.

"What's the time?"

"Almost four." Neil said and stretched on the bed, lazily. She toyed her fingers through her hair. "You were wonderful. Do you have a girlfriend?"

"You want some coffee?" He asked in reply.

"You'll make it?"

He nodded and walked off towards the kitchen.

When he returned with two cups, she was fully dressed.

"Come to the balcony," Neil invited her and placed the cups on the cane table.

She came out and gasped, "Wow! Look at the sea! Great for an outing, eh?"

Neil smiled, "Here, take." He handed her a cup and sat down. She sat opposite him and crossed her brown bare legs. Her white mini skirt barely reached her thighs.

She sipped on the hot liquid and looked at him. "You are a nice boy. How did you get mixed up with Remo?"

"I am not *mixed up* with Remo. He's a friend and I am thankful that he let me stay with him for two months. Now that I have found a job, thanks to you, I'll move out into a pad of my own."

Juhi suddenly laughed, "You think that's easy? Finding a pad in Mumbai is easy?"

"Let's see. I'll start looking around from tomorrow."

"You can move in with me, " she offered sincerely. "I live in a two bed-roomed flat alone. I'll keep you very happy. Then we can live like husband and wife," she smiled mischievously.

Neil tilted his neck and looked at her, "You like all this?"

She got a little flustered. "Why not? I get paid for it."

"Then I'd pose a problem. You won't be able to bring in your customers."

She raised her eyebrows. "'Customer' is a word I don't like. I prefer 'Friends'." She smiled wryly. "Umm... let's see... we can work out something... Maybe when you leave for office I'll call them over."

"Why do you want to go through all this for me?"

She looked at him from an angle, "Because I like you."

Neil looked away and sipped on his coffee. "Thanks. But, no thanks. Let's see what I can do. Then if I get desperate I'll call on you."

She had finished her cup. She placed it on the table and stretched her arms above her head. "You know remarkable tricks in bed. Where did you learn them from? Girlfriend? From books?"

Neil looked down. And then at her. "I'm surprised, considering the kind of life you lead. What can *I* teach you? You are a master yourself." He smiled at her dryly.

Juhi became serious and her small eyes bore into his. "Nobody has ever spoken to me like this. I don't like it."

Neil shrugged, "That's surprising. Somebody should have. You do not have that dearth of money that you'd go to bed with every man you come across and get paid for it."

This time she was angry. Really mad. She sat up straight and hissed dangerously. "You know you are crossing your limits. Just because I like you and put you up in a fat job in my uncle's travel agency in two days flat, you think you can dictate the way I live?"

Neil looked away. Droplets of water were pouring from the heavens. The rain was a light shower. "I don't mean to hurt you, Juhi. But I don't want any of my friends to associate with something they don't like." He looked at her. "And I have found out that you don't really like it."

Juhi stared at him. Then stood up. "I have to go. I have an appointment."

She picked up her purse and quickly left the flat. She stood near the lift waiting for it to come up while she combed her hair. She ran a dark lipstick on her lips, stealing a quick glance behind — scared that he'll come out.

She came down the lift and started her green Maruti. She took to Juhu Tara Road and turned on Bon Jovi on her music system. The droplets had stopped falling and the road was slippery. Traffic was heavy despite it being a Sunday.

She didn't have much to do if she got back home. There was no Remo and hence, no party tonight. She pondered. Where did she want to go? To Barry? And get a customer fixed up for the night? She had 10 grands in her purse. She could well relax for a few days. She could go off for a holiday in Madh Island. Alone? *With Neil?*

She was shocked at the last thought. Did she like him that much? He seemed to be such a breath of fresh air. He seemed such an anchor. She felt he was invincible despite the low profile he kept. She felt he would soon put her in a lot of dilemma about her life. *Was she falling in love with him?*

Suddenly she wanted to turn back. Neil was all alone. He would be for the rest of the evening. He didn't know many people in Mumbai.

She let go of the thought. She was rushing things. She had to understand her own life first.

Neil had almost finished the letter he was writing to Mahamaya. He spoke about the job and how good Remo was. '...I am getting a salary of 12 thousand. I'll soon be able to pay back Baba.

'How's everybody at home? Ma, you are the crux of the family. Please take care of yourself and everybody. Love, Neilu.'

However much he wanted he couldn't bring himself to talk about Tuli. He thought of writing to her. But that may prove dangerous again. He desperately wanted to talk to her. Meet her. Write to her. Know how she was.

The phone rang. Must be Remo. He had gone to Goa on an 'official' tour.

"Hello?"

"Hi, this is Juhi."

"Oh hi! What's up?"

"What were you doing?"

"Nothing much. I was... er...relaxing."

"Can we go out for dinner? I want to show you around Mumbai night life."

Neil thought for a moment. He didn't exactly feel like going out. But he had no bindings.

Juhi was speaking, "I want to take you to a favorite joint of mine. What do you say?"

"Fine. But ... er..." He was thinking of money.

"The evening's on me." Juhi read his thoughts. He was not sure why she was so interested in him. She was his boss's mistress, whom she referred to as 'Barry Uncle'. He didn't want to upset her. His job was very vital.

Juhi was saying, "I'll pick you up in an hour."

"Where are you?"

"I am in Bandra. Why?"

"I'm coming over. Give me the address."

"But you don't know anything about Mumbai."

"I'll find out. Give me the address."

CHAPTER 13

Mumbai, April 1995

Two months later Tuli's letter arrived.

Juhi was out with Neil practically every weekend, sometimes even during the weekdays when Neil got off early. Neil hadn't shifted to a personal pad as Remo never allowed him to. Remo wasn't the kind to get attached to anyone. He had seen too much of life. But this boy was different. However, he wasn't prepared for him to steal his girlfriend.

It was a Friday and Neil was sunk in work. His colleague, Sonia stuck on and helped him out. When he came out of the office at nine with Sonia, he saw Juhi standing against her parked car.

"Hi, you didn't inform me?"

"I didn't want to disturb you," she smiled and then looked with stabbing eyes at Sonia. Sonia said, "Okay Neil, see you," and walked off.

He was at a loss for words. They had planned to go back home together since she helped him so much.

Juhi opened the car door for him. "Thanks," he sat inside. She started up the machine.

"You are quite popular, huh?" she jested.

Neil smiled. He knew what she meant. She took a sharp bend into the main road.

"Sorry I messed up your evening. You wanted to go out with her, didn't you?"

"No, nothing of that sort."

"She's quite a beauty, isn't she?"

Neil looked at her. "Where are we going?"

Juhi fell silent.

"You know Barry uncle's a little suspicious about us?" She said after a while.

"So why are you risking all this? Even Remo's upset you're not paying him enough attention."

"Fuck them galore!" Her eyes brimmed with a surprising hatred for them. Neil decided not to speak about them anymore. He knew she was going to take him to a new discotheque this evening. For the past two months she had taken him all over Mumbai. She had spent a few thousands on him and wanted to spend more. He realized she liked him. But he didn't know why. He was neither satisfying her financially, nor sexually. They never touched each other after their first encounter in Remo's flat two months back. She never insisted on it either.

She turned onto Marine Drive and then headed for the beach. She slowed her car once she reached there and rolled it by the thick boundary walls that separated the sea from the city. It was nearing ten and traffic was becoming thinner. The high wall of Marine Drive was, however, teeming with couples sitting and gorging their souls on the sea. For once you sat there with your back to the city you forgot the reality and what's behind you. You drowned your soul into the slashing waves, wild and fierce, against this man-made obstruction.

Juhi parked her car. Was this a parking zone? Neil looked around. She took out the car keys and got out. Neil followed suit, without any questions and locked his door. Juhi came around and held his hand.

"Come I'll show you something."

She discovered an empty stretch on the wall and turned to Neil, "Put me on it." She extended her arms like a baby. Neil held her under her arms and jerked her up on top of the wall. *He remembered something. His heart turned into a lump.*

He sat beside her. Instantly the sea captured their attention. The incessant waves slashing on the wall created an intoxication that filled Neil's soul up to the brim.

Juhi spoke first after a while of silence. "I've never felt like this before."

Neil turned to her. He was far away in his thoughts. He tried to comprehend what she meant.

She looked at the sea, "I am neck-deep in an emotion for you. I don't feel like earning the way I earn. I want to start a respectable life." She turned to him, reached out and held his hand.

His first instinct was to withdraw the hand. Then he kept calm. He had suspected something like this. But he never believed himself. Now he began to.

He held back her hand and said, 'Juhi, you've been a wonderful help. I wouldn't have been able to set a foot in Mumbai without you. But aren't you rushing things? Let's be friends. We barely know each other."

Juhi leant her head on his shoulders. He stiffened. "I don't care whether I am rushing things. I don't want to know anything more about you. I don't care for anybody else."

Neil pushed her back, "Let's go." He felt like fleeing.

Juhi smiled, "You mean, let's go home?"

"No. *I* want to go home. I'm expecting a call." He cooked it up.

She looked at him with hurt eyes. He didn't care. He stepped down and held out his hand for her. Unwillingly, she got down.

"You go safely." Neil said, once they reached the car. "I'll take an auto." He ushered her inside.

She wanted to protest. But an invincible look in his eyes made her stop. She sat at the wheels.

"When will I see you?"

"I'll call you," he patted her cheeks.

She drove away. Neil felt he saw her eyes brimming with tears.

He reached home in the dead of night. Remo was awake, drinking and watching a serial on TV.

"Hi! What's up? Out with Juhi again?"

Neil didn't speak. He walked into the bathroom. Something in Remo's voice warned him. He showered and came out in his shorts.

"You find that bitch so irresistible?"

"Remo," Neil sighed. "You're not feeling well. Why don't you go to sleep?"

Remo laughed, "Ha! Ha! You think she's going to give you a kingdom? She'll suck your juice out and then set you free."

Neil sat down on the sofa and switched channels.

Remo gulped down the rest of the drinks and stood up, wobbly. "Oh! By the way, there's a letter for you. From someone called 'Tuli'." He waddled into his room and banged the door shut.

Neil sat numb for a few seconds. Then his mind raced. A letter from Tuli? Where? Where did Remo keep it? His eyes raced across the room. From the center table to the dining table and the top of the cabinet. Nothing... he rushed into his room. The study table, the bed, on top of the cupboard. Nothing. He was about to knock on Remo's door, when he saw it!

On top of the TV!

He strode slowly towards it. His brain rushed but his legs refused to move. It was as though Tuli herself was standing so near him, yet so far away...

He tore open the letter.

'Dear Neil, Neilu, Sweetheart, how are the girls in Mumbai?...'

This was Tuli! This was her magic! Look at the way she threw up life into air as if it belonged to someone else.

'... I am FINE!' and drew a smiling face beside it. Neil smiled. 'Calcutta is beginning to hot up. You know, how we celebrated our anniversary? Soumen threw a party at the *thakurdalan*. Imagine, we cut a cake and drank in the *thakurdalan* and Ma didn't say a thing...' Neil's smile vanished. Maybe things *were* falling into place there. That's what she hinted at... "of course *Baba* and *kakas* didn't like it. I guess it was right. What do you say?

'How's Remo? Did you mention to him about me? Have you found a friend? Oh by the way, your son AAKASH is kicking wildly in my stomach. I think he's going after his father. Wild! Poor Soumen, he thinks it's his baby. And is celebrating wildly...!'

COME AGAIN!

Neil thought he misunderstood and read again. '*…your son AAKASH is kicking wildly… Soumen thinks it's his baby…*'

His world began to spin! The ground beneath him began to slip away!! *His SON?!! Tuli is pregnant with his son?!!*

He sunk down in the sofa.

"*My son?*" he pronounced the two words aloud to make himself believe it. *My son?* Tuli never mentioned it to him. He quickly calculated back. He left Calcutta in November. The last time they went to bed was in August. August 24. He remembered the day. Which meant in November she was three months pregnant already? She knew! She didn't tell him then? If she did, perhaps he wouldn't have had to come to Mumbai alone. He would have brought her along, taken a braver decision…

My son!

He held his head. "*…You must be wondering why I've become so serious, so sane. I'll let you know one day… not now…*" He suddenly remembered the Mahalaya day. She *had* had intentions of telling him later on. But then decided against it. Now when he's settled down in Mumbai, she let him know. And in what a way! As an off-hand information at the end!

Tuli…

He got up and paced the room. He read the letter over and over again to make sure he didn't misunderstand. Then he sat down and poured himself a large whiskey, from the bottle left around by Remo. He gulped it down on the rocks. He shook and burnt from within. He wanted to get drunk. For the first time in his life he wanted to cry. He had taken so much pain without a single tear. But now that happiness burst into his domain, he wanted to cry. He poured himself another. And gulped it down. It hit him like a bullet. He plopped down on the sofa and closed his eyes. The drinks hit his head. It began raising him into ether. He forgot everything else.

Aakash! She must be full eight months pregnant now. Full size. Tears rolled down his cheeks. What did she look like? Quite a cartoon, huh? Aakash must be quite big. Who did he look like? Come on. It can be a 'she' for all you knew. What would I name her if it's a 'she'? Hmmm… he smiled. Maybe 'Toofan'. Toofan in Bengali meant a hurricane. She would be another hurricane like Tuli. *Tiny hands and minutest feet.* He laughed aloud. Tuli had said so. She wasn't going to die before having her baby. He'd play with the small hands, hold it in his large ones … Tears burst out of his eyes and gushed down his cheeks as he laughed… laughed to himself. And his world burst into a rainbow, a kaleidoscope! He suddenly wanted to live! Fly across the sky! Jump from a parachute... wade through the deepest ocean. He suddenly wanted to scream to the world and say *"I love you, Tuli! I love you, life!!"* and run all the way into her arms!

CHAPTER 14

Neil began preparing for the battle. It was as though life itself had walked up to him and was saying: *"Hold me Neil, please take me in your arms..."*

He couldn't flee anymore. He was taking swift decisions. He had to find a flat first. An apartment. A domain. Any small one would do. He'd bring Tuli and the baby here. It's going to be tough. Terrible. They'd probably be crushed under the weight of problems. But he'd survive. And help Tuli survive. Life was there, smiling for him. He had no other way out.

He had to face the Roy family after that. That would be, however, less difficult. It all depended on her. And her agreeing to the decision.

He had to first find a flat. And then take a train, a plane, fly, *run* to Calcutta.

He phoned home the next morning. He had to be very careful. Mahamaya picked up the phone.

"Ma?"

"Neilu! How are you? You haven't got my letter?"

"No. Not yet. How's *Baba*? How's his blood sugar problem?"

"Better. Have you found a flat for yourself?"

"Not yet. How's Tuli? Heard she's... not well?"

There was a small silence. Then she asked, "Where did you hear it from?"

"Er... from a friend of her college who came here. I met her accidentally."

"Oh, she's fine." She was harsh.

"Is she around? Can I speak to her?"

There was a big silence on the other end.

"Ma please, it's very urgent."

She was silent. Then she said, "Okay."

He waited with bated breath.

"Hello?" Tuli!

He couldn't speak for a while.

"Hello! Are you there?"

"Yes," he whispered. "How are you?"

"Fine. How are you?"

"Tuli... I got your letter... Aakash... is it true?"

There was a pause. "Yes."

"I love you Tuli. I love you so much. I'm coming over. Will you marry me, Tuli?"

She laughed. And sniffed. He realized she was crying. "Don't cry anymore, dear. There's not going to be any more tears for us. I am bringing you over."

There was complete silence except for soft sniffs.

"Just wait for me. I am going to find a flat. And then bring you both over. And then we'll get married. Wait for me, Tuli. Hang on for me."

"Yes..." she whispered. "Come fast... "

Come fast... come fast... That was all he could remember after they hung up the phone. *I'm coming Tuli...*

He decided to speak to Remo about the flat.

CHAPTER 15

Remo came back that night with high fever.

Neil had left office in the afternoon. He walked barefoot over the sand on the beach for a long time. The beach was teeming with people. The *chowpatty* looked raided as the sun slowly sunk into a stretch of clouds just above the ashen ocean. It was going to rain again today. Little slum boys were building sand castles near the shore, which got wiped away by the waves. Neil watched an immense sadistic pleasure in their eyes as they clapped their hands every time their dream domains got washed away. They built it again and again it got washed away. Neil thought it was weird.

He came back home with two *rumali rotis* [36] and *tadka* [37] in an earthen pot. His dinner. He showered, changed and sat by the TV eating his dinner from the newspaper packet itself. He was famished and after finishing two *rotis* as big as napkins, he felt he could have had two more.

Remo walked in just as he was washing himself.

"Hi!" he wished cheerfully. Remo looked up. His face was dark and his eyes were red.

"Hey, are you all right?"

Remo nodded his head in negative and waddled, almost falling off. Neil quickly ran to his side and held him. He was burning with fever!

"Oh my god! When did this happen?"

He led Remo into his room and made him lie down. "Let's see if I have a paracetamol."

He found one and gave it to him with a glass of water.

"You want me to call a doctor?"

Remo shook his head. He swallowed the tablet and plopped back to bed. Neil was worried. Remo couldn't even speak properly. He didn't have a thermometer. Anyway, the paracetamol will bring down the fever. Hopefully.

He sat on the sofa switching channels. His mind was clouded with so many thoughts that he felt he couldn't sleep that night. He'd never be able to sleep again!

He heard a sound and rushed inside. He switched on the light. Remo was up and was bent over on the side of the bed. Smelly liquid had spilt all over the floor! He was panting as another thick splurge of liquid rushed out from his mouth.

Neil rushed into the kitchen and got a glass of water. He climbed onto the bed and held him. Remo had been crying. Tears were rolling down his cheeks.

Neil gave him the water. "It's okay, you'll feel better now." Then climbed down and got a hanky from his drawer. He wiped off Remo's mouth and eyes and took the glass from his hands.

"Sorry," Remo spoke at last. "I'll clean it tomorrow. I can't today. You close the door and leave me."

"It's okay. You sleep. You'll definitely feel better tomorrow." Neil held his head and helped him lie down. He went into the kitchen and found a mop. He took a bucket of water from the bathroom. Then came back into the room and wiped off all the smelly, yellow liquid — from the floor, the side table and from the walls. There was not a tinge of nausea in him in doing so. All he felt was, leaving Remo with all this mess around was the most inhuman thing one could do.

The latter was oblivious to all this. He was fast asleep. Neil then pulled the covers over his legs, switched on the fan on low, switched off the light, closed the door and went out. He hoped he would be better the next morning.

The next morning Neil awoke with Remo calling him. He jumped up. He was late for office!

Then he saw Remo. He had made two cups of coffee and gave him one cup.

"'Morning!" he said.

"How're you feeling?"

Remo waved his hand in the air. "Alright." Then he said, "You cleaned all that?" He sat beside him on the bed.

Neil sipped on the liquid.

Remo smiled at him. And sipped his coffee.

Neil turned, "What's the time?"

"Eight-thirty."

"What… oh my god!" he jumped out of the bed. His office started at nine!

"Neil," called out Remo. Neil stopped. "Forget office today."

"What do you mean? I have piles of work."

"Forget it. I'll call up Barry."

He was insistent and Neil felt that he had something in mind. He came back to the bed. His mind still racing to get ready for office.

Remo took out a packet of cigarettes from the pocket of his shorts and lit two and handed Neil one. Neil walked over and opened the door of the balcony. He walked out. The sea was wonderful. The sun was up and a few slum boys were wading in the sea. They were small specs but he could perceive the energy that they had daylong with their association with the sea.

Remo joined him. Neil sipped on the liquid and asked, "What happened? How did you catch the fever?"

"I don't know. Maybe something I ate."

They leant over the railings. "Yeah, I guessed so. You had acidity."

"You cleaned all that. How could you?"

Remo laughed, trying to make himself believe Neil actually did it.

"Why, do you always clean your own mess? Nobody ever did it for you?"

He nodded.

"Your mother must have done it."

"Yah, that's long time ago. You know I felt very funny when I saw the mess cleaned up. I felt you could be a friend. I could depend on you."

"I am a friend," Neil looked away.

Remo nodded. "I never took you as one." He looked at him, "Sorry, and thanks." He smiled. Neil smiled and hugged him.

"There're no 'sorry' and 'thanks' in friendship."

He sat down on the chair. "Hey, I wanted to find a flat for myself. Can you help me?"

"A flat?" Remo looked disappointed. "You are having problems staying here?"

"No, no..." Neil stopped "Er... I think I have to move now. Now that I've got a job." He smiled, trying to uplift his mood. "We had that kind of pact, remember?"

"Yes, but so soon? You can stay here longer if you want. If you feel an obligation, pay me a rent."

"No." Neil was thinking. Should he tell him? Maybe he'd understand then. He couldn't possibly bring Tuli and Aakash into this flat where call girls walked in and out and drunken friends stayed overnight.

"You don't understand. I plan to settle down." He said very slowly.

"You mean..." Remo's face was off color. "Juhi?"

"No, no," Neil laughed. "Juhi's just a friend."

"Then?"

Neil sighed. And looked into the sky. Dark clouds had vanished and white clouds sailed across. The sky was an azure blue. The air smelt flowery and romantic. *Nothing could go wrong anymore...*

"I have someone." He let out. Remo was silent. "I plan to marry her."

"In Calcutta?" He guessed.

Neil nodded.

Remo smiled, "Hey you cheeky son-of-a-bitch. All the while you made me feel Juhi was pinning you down. *Saala! Chhupe rustam,* tell me, what is she like?"

What's she like? Neil smiled. He could talk about her for hours. But this was not the time. He had to hurry things. He had to speak to a lawyer too.

"She's... a nice person." He framed a definition. And then wasn't sure. Was the definition befitting her, was she a nice person, considering she was carrying her brother-in-law's child? Cheating on her husband? He felt bitterness and realized that he was testing himself deliberately. Thinking from the society's point of view and trying to fathom whether he still loved her or not.

"Hey! Come back!" Remo snapped his fingers in front of him.

Neil smiled. Remo sang aloud, "*Saala, mein to baaja bajaunga...* I'll dance. I'll sing.." and he began dancing his elbows.

"Hey, not so fast. There won't be any pomp and ceremony." He decided to tell him. "We'll marry in private. She's going to carry a newborn baby."

"What?!" Remo was aghast! "Your baby?"

Neil nodded.

"And she's not married yet?"

Neil shook his head. "She's married to my brother."

Remo looked around. Completely confused. "Wait a second. She's married to your brother... which meant, she's your *bhabi*." He waited and cringed his eyes at him "You are having an affair with your *bhabi*?"

Neil nodded.

"She's carrying your child?"

He nodded again.

"She's divorced your brother?"

"No."

"You plan to get her divorced and then marry her, with the child?"

He nodded.

Remo threw himself on the backrest of the chair. "This is blasphemous!"

Neil smiled. *Wait till you meet her.* You'll know what blasphemy is!

"Now you understand why I'm looking for a flat?"

Remo considered for a moment. "I still think we all can fit into this flat. Anyway, since you want to start life afresh... humm... let's see, I'll speak to Hassan*bhai*."

"No," Neil cut short. "I don't want any obligations from Hassan*bhai*."

"Come on, it's not an obligation. He's an influential man. He'll get you a good flat."

"What would you have done if you hadn't known him?"

"I... I don't know anybody... in Mumbai..." It was clear that Remo was totally dependent on the mafia man.

Neil looked away, "Forget it. I'll look for it myself."

He sifted through the ads in the next day's newspaper and made a few phone calls. Some were befitting his imagination but not his pocket and some were not fitting his imagination at all. He decided to let go of his imagination.

He found a decent one-room flat in Umarkhadi. It was way off the sea and his office. *He's going to miss the sea.*

He paid two months' rent and asked Remo if he could arrange for the 'advance'. The 'advance' meant a fat deposit to the owner, in case the tenant fled not having paid rent. Remo clicked his tongue, "I told you Hassan*bhai* could fix up something better. Now where do I get fifty thousand bucks?"

"You throw up some more money on Juhi and you'll end up being a pauper." Neil was angry.

Remo flared up. "Juhi's my business, okay?"

Neil became quiet and left the room.

They didn't speak for two days. It was apparent that the tension was killing Neil. Or he never usually gets so angry with anyone. He decided to say 'sorry' that evening.

The day had not been bad. As he entered office there was an intercom call from Barry. "Come in Neil, I want to see you."

"Sure," he hurried inside.

"Sit down," said the big, sloppy man. Neil hated the way his belly moved and his shirt carelessly fell out of his trousers. Why couldn't he do a bit of a workout? They were all doing so in Mumbai. And Juhi? How could she sleep with this man? Money, I guess.

Sonia, his PA was scribbling something. She hurried off. Barry had often tried to get close to this girl on several occasions. But the petite girl had a mind of steel. She managed to steer him clear at the same time keep up her job. Neil and she were great friends. She shared her lunch often with him. Lately, he began to realize she was bringing lunch for two. Maybe she didn't have enough after sharing with him, Neil thought and refused her on two occasions. She never insisted, but she was hurt. He said, "Okay, let's make a deal. You bring lunch for me, I'll pay you." Again the hurt look in her eyes. He had decided to let her take charge of his lunch. This happened just a day back.

"Juhi says you need a flat?"

Neil was surprised. Did he mention it to Juhi? He must have. Or Remo might have.

"Yes. But I've got one."

"Where?"

"In Umerkhadi."

"Umerkhadi?" he shook his head. "I have an empty flat at Versova. I can rent it out to you."

"With my salary?" Neil smiled.

"You pay me three thousand."

Neil laughed. Three thousand for a flat in Versova, one of the most posh areas of Mumbai? Barry must be joking.

"You're joking?"

His boss looked angry. The fat man pulled up to full stature. "Take it or leave it."

"Sorry," Neil looked at him. "I'll let you know." Then he thought for a moment. "Can you loan me fifty thousand right now?"

"Fifty thousand?"

"Yes. I need it."

Barry nodded, "Hmm... planning to settle down?"

Neil didn't know what he knew. How much he should tell him. He didn't want Juhi to know about all this now. He wanted to tell her himself.

"I might want to settle down." He cut in. His eyes said, *It's my business.*

Barry understood. "Let's see, if I can arrange something."

Neil came out and walked into his work enclosure. He sat down at the computer.

"You are having an affair with Juhi?"

He jumped and looked behind him. Sonia. He let out a sigh. She sat down on a chair. He smiled, "You scared me."

She looked at him, "Are you?"

He felt like telling her, *It's none of your business,* but wasn't sure whether that would make him lose out on all the sumptuous lunches.

He looked at her, "Why are people so curious about me?"

She smiled and looked down. She was in a dress that revealed her cleavages. Neil felt slightly uncomfortable.

"You *are* that kind of a person," she shrugged.

It was a compliment, and Neil liked it. He looked back at the computer screen.

"You still haven't told me whether you are having an affair with her or not."

He looked down. Then at her. "Why would I tell you?" He decided to risk those lunches.

"Because I am a friend. And I'm going to tell you that she's not a nice girl. You know…" she crossed her brows and lowered her voice. "'She sleeps around… you are a nice guy. Don't get involved with her."

Neil hid a desperate urge to laugh. He decided to tell her what she wanted to hear, "Don't worry, nothing will happen to me," he smiled and said in a low, sexy voice. She blushed.

The gods that night swore that Neil must die!

CHAPTER 16

Mumbai, May 4, 1995

The day sure was going great guns. Neil whistled as he entered the flat. It was empty. Remo wasn't back yet. There was a note on the fridge. 'Your mother called. She asked you to call back. She said it's urgent.'

It was past ten in the evening. He looked at his watch and then rushed for the lift. The STD booth downstairs may still be open. He didn't want to make a call from Remo's phone without saying 'Sorry' to Remo first.

It was! Thank God! The booth man was locking up his cash box. About to close up.

Neil rushed in. "Can I?"

The man waved his hand and reopened his cash box. Neil dialed. The machine seemed to be taking an eternity to reciprocate. At last the phone rang at the other end.

"Hello?" It was Mahamaya.

"Hello. Ma? How's everything? What happened? Why did you call?"

There was a deadly silence on the other end. Neil thought she couldn't hear him. "Ma?" he repeated, "Ma, why..."

"Tuli is ill... serious." Her voice filtered through like a deadly warning. "She's contacted jaundice, at this last stage. She's in the hospital. The doctor..." She stopped. As if she was changing her mind and was about to tell him all was a joke and *Aakash was actually*

155

born! "You come down. She needs you." She added, *"As soon as possible."*

"I'm coming. Right away." Neil's first reaction was that her mother had understood their relationship. As for Tuli being seriously ill, of course, nothing is going to happen to her. Nothing.

He paid the bill.

So many women have jaundice. He knew someone in college who had jaundice when she was pregnant. She recovered. Maybe Tuli's bilirubin is higher. So what? Calcutta doctors are experts. And it's almost the twenty-first century. Nothing's going to happen to her.

He rushed up the stairs. Then remembered the lift and came down. He pressed the button for the lift. The door opened. He pressed 12. The lift was taking eons to ascend. Was there a late night flight to Calcutta? He had to consult Remo. He reached his floor and rushed into his flat. It was still dark.

Remo. He needed Remo. Somehow, he felt, he couldn't spare a minute. Where could he be? With Juhi? With Ibrahim Hassan? He had Juhi's mobile number.

He dialed. Shit! The machine was switched off. That girl! She must be in bed with someone. With whom? Remo? Where were they?

He looked at Remo's phone book lying beside the phone. He turned the pages to 'H'.

CHAPTER 17

"You want some beer sir?" Neil looked up. The girl was beautiful. Must be one of Hassan's girls.

"No." he looked down from the oval window of the private aircraft. The sky was clearing up. The sun would be up any moment. The clouds floated by like he was in a dreamland.

He had been right. Remo was with Hassan.

"Remo, I need you. I need to speak to you…"

"What happened?"

"Tuli's in the hospital."

"Who's Tuli?"

"Oh!" he had forgotten to tell him her name. "I spoke to you about her…"

"Oh… why? What happened to her?"

"She's got jaundice. She's serious. I have to rush to Calcutta right now. The baby…"

"What happened to the baby?" Remo's voice was serious.

"Nothing. I don't know…" He realized his voice was cracking. "I don't know anything. Please help me get a booking on a plane. There are flights at night, right?"

Remo hesitated in saying a 'No'.

"You come over. I'm sending a car right away." He knew Hassan*bhai* would fix up something.

Remo put down the phone and turned to Hassan*bhai*. He was talking business with Vasant. He rushed to his side. And spoke something in his ear.

Neil packed a few clothes. His credit card and all the money he had. He needed more. He'd ask Remo for some. He rushed downstairs.

A blue Maruti came after an endless wait for over 20 minutes. The driver stuck his head out. "Neil *saab*?"

"Yes." He rushed inside it. The car took off.

It crossed the entire city to reach Pali Hill, one of the most posh areas of Mumbai. A spate of remarkable bungalows lined on each side of the road. They had high walls and splendid gates with dome-shaped or pear-shaped lights fitted on the entrances. One of the gates swung open when the driver honked.

The driveway was lit dimly with lights hidden among the grass. The lawn was softly lit with a few lampposts placed around erratically and it appeared an unearthly green. A massive swing was at the center of the lawn with white garden chairs around it.

The car came to a halt under a white portico. In fact the entire grandeur of the house was in white. The driver came out and opened the gate for a dazed Neil.

He climbed up wide steps leading to a heavy, ornate wooden carved door. He didn't notice, but the door had carvings, which were facsimiles of the Ajanta Caves. He had seen so many of these houses in movies, but never really believed one actually existed. A man in starched, white uniform came up to him and folded his hands.

"Namaste, come upstairs, Sir."

The stairs leading up were embedded with colored stones on the sides and swung around a heavily furnished enormous hall. Neil glanced around and he saw a small, blue swimming pool with a white statue of a nude woman having a bath in a fountain that was flowing down a pot she held over her shoulders. A sharp disparity of blue velvet sofas was placed all around the pool that was complemented with dark brown ebony furniture and a dark red carpet. The pool had a rock garden on one side, near the wall, where a statue of a nude mermaid sat tying her hair into a bun above her head. Small, carved, ebony tables and short, fat, sofas were strewn around. On one end of the hall there was a round, glass dance floor with soft lights beneath. Concealed lighting made the room appear ethereal.

Remo greeted him on top of the stairs.

"Come, meet Hassan*bhai*."

He led him into another sprawling room, which could be supposed to be Hassan's personal living room. The furniture here was more relaxed. It was oriental, with low Gujarati sofas and tables. A mattress with *gurjari* cushions, from Gujarat, was placed at a corner, with soft illumination throughout the room. A man in his late fifties sat on one of the sofas. He was attired in a dressing gown and held a cigar between his fingers. He had his legs crossed, which was clad in a pair of stark white pajamas. He wore a pair of oriental slip-ons Neil had never seen anywhere before.

Two glasses of colored drinks were placed in a Gujarati low table in front of him. A wad of papers lay on it too. Another man, in his late forties, attired in a safari suit and wearing rimless golden glasses sat on another sofa. They both looked threatening. Neil felt a little nervous.

Hassan examined him in seconds and then stood up. "Please come in." he waved his hand and showed him a sofa to his right. Remo ushered him in and they both sat on the large sofa, Remo sitting closer to Hassan.

"Yes," Hassan cleared his throat. "Remo told me your problem."

Then he waited and looked at him. "But apparently, you don't want to take any help from me. Why?"

Neil pressed his lips and looked hard at Remo. Remo smiled as if to say, 'Hey, come on, he won't mind.'

"No…" Neil cleared his throat. "No, I mean…"

"I understand. But now that you are in trouble, you will." He said categorically, which sounded sarcastic.

Neil sighed and looked around. Two men were posted at the door. Black revolvers were peeping from their pockets.

He felt trapped. Hassan was rubbing in the fact that he had to take his help even though he didn't want to. He opened his mouth to say something. Hassan spoke.

"You won't get any flights — until day after tomorrow." He waited for his reaction. They were frantic. Desperate. Devoid of thinking logically. Day after tomorrow may be too late!

"I can hire you a private aircraft, if you so wish."

A private aircraft?! Hire him?! Neil thought about the cost.

Hassan spoke, "You don't have to pay me anything now. But I'll give you an offer. You come back and help me out a bit. You know, assist Remo in his work." He smiled for the first time. A gold tooth sparkled. "I am getting old. I need young, energetic people like you to join my business."

Neil was shocked! This man was buying him! He looked away. He was thinking fast. He was being drawn into the underworld, which he had avoided for so long. He had no choice. Nothing was more important to him than Tuli.

He took a decision.

"Okay."

Even Remo was surprised. He had expected Neil to storm out of the room, at best refuse. But he was surprised to see how important Tuli was to him. More important than himself or his own principles.

The six-seater private aircraft took off from the Santa Cruz airport at 4 a.m. with two other men who were to visit Calcutta that day.

The clouds cleared and Neil saw the sun.

"Please tie your seatbelts. We are landing at Dumdum airport."

Neil looked down. He saw a familiar labyrinth of coconut trees. He was home!

CHAPTER 18

Calcutta, May 5 1995

The imposing domain seemed unearthly quiet. Neil rushed in and threw his suitcase somewhere. He rushed upstairs. The house was sleeping. *Dada*'s room was locked. All other rooms were closed and sleepy. Everything was in order. As if nothing happened. Maybe Tuli was well. Maybe the baby was already born. *His baby...* He saw his mother, coming out of the prayer room.

Mahamaya saw him. She was aghast! "Neilu... so early... how could you come so fast?"

"How's Tuli?"

Mahamaya cast her eyes down.

"Ma, how's Tuli? Where is she?" He walked towards her threateningly.

She looked up. "She's in Dr Bhattacharya's Nursing home."

She was alive!

Neil turned and raced!

"Don't go now. The visiting hours are from..."

He didn't hear the rest. He was out on the streets.

He hailed a taxi and said, "Bhowanipore and *fast*!"

He sat on the edge of the seat with a ready fifty-rupee note in hand. His mind raced. She was in the hospital. Was she alright? Was he overreacting? Did Ma hide anything from him? He didn't want to think about the baby. The thought gave him a jab in the stomach. He tried to clear his cloudy thoughts. Was jaundice in pregnancy fatal? He was tempted to ask someone. Whom? The taxi driver? He wanted the information. Maybe his wife had jaundice in pregnancy and had *lived*...

Had lived?!! Why was he thinking Tuli won't live? Of course she would. The prediction... Fuck all bullshit predictions! And anyway, twenty is no age to die. She had natural body resistance and this was her first pregnancy. He thought clinically and heaved a short sigh. No. He was overreacting. Of course, she'll live. And their baby? Would it be a boy or a girl? It didn't matter. All that mattered was that it would have tiny hands and minute feet that he was going to hold. And the baby would wail. And feed on Tuli's breast. A faint smile lit up his face. He missed her very much. A lump rose from his stomach up to his throat. He pushed it down. Why should he cry? He would take her to Mumbai, go through all that painful process of separation and divorce. And then marry her. Remo would be his best man. Who could be a better friend? He gave him a lakh of rupees when he left Mumbai. *And Hassan?* He felt like blowing off a kiss to Hassan. Let tongues wag, but a friend in need is a friend indeed. Hassan had helped him wonderfully in his worst crisis. He felt his hatred for the man slowly melt. Okay. So he'll work for him erratically. He'd have the whole world in his hands. Why did he care?

The taxi took a sharp right turn as Neil directed for it to stop in front of a white building. "Popular Nursing Home," it said.

He handed the money to the driver and didn't look back for the change. He ran inside.

Soumen, Tuli's mother and uncle sat in various seats scattered in the lobby.

"Neilu!" Soumen's voice was surprisingly warm. He came and hugged his brother. One guesses at times of crisis personal animosities melt. But Neil wasn't thinking of that. *He was reading his expression.*

"How's she?"

Soumen looked away. Neil turned him to face him. And Soumen's expression gave away!

"What do you mean?!" Where are the doctors? I am taking her out of here. Where is she?" He didn't realize his voice was raising an octave.

Soumen looked at Tuli's mother, as if for help. She sat lifeless looking blank at Neil, streams of tears running down her cheeks. Her uncle came up to Neil.

"Son," he was composed. "She's had a hepatitis failure. The baby's dead already." He broke down. "Tuli... my daughter..." He shook his head and hugged Neil.

Neil didn't believe any of them. "Where is she?"

"First floor. ICU."

ICU?!! His steps, which had started to run up the stairs, became slightly slower. He caught up with them and *ran*.

He leaped up the stairs onto the first floor. Left...? Right...? He saw the deadly warnings in red 'ICU. KEEP OUT'.

He threw open the door. There she was! Pale... lifeless... merged with the bed... a tube stuck into her nose... and another into her arms. In fact there were so many tubes Neil couldn't count. She wasn't breathing! *Was she dead?!* No. He saw her chest rise and drop. And again a moment's stillness. Then the chest rose again and fell.

He rushed to her side despite one nurse asking him not to. He must have shouted something inane to her, because she rushed out, pale-faced. Good. Now he could be alone with her.

He held her hand delicately and ran a palm over her forehead. Suddenly her hand moved beneath his. He looked at it. *It was alive! She was alive!* She understood his touch. She was trying to hold his hand. He turned to look at her face.

He was looking at a pair of open eyes!

Yellow with jaundice, yet beautiful, black and alive! He smiled. She attempted one, despite the tubes. Then her eyes filled up with tears. A big drop fell down her temple and she slowly shook her head.

He tried to speak. Instead he bent down and kissed the corner of her lips. Then he raised her hand and kissed it. He could only say, "It's okay. I've come. You're going to be all right. Just hang on."

She looked at him with wide eyes with one teardrop running down after another.

And then she closed her eyes!

Neil told her softly, "Sleep, sweetheart. I am going to take you home. My home."

He turned to face a crowd. He recognized a few — Soumen, Tuli's uncle, an aged man, a nurse, a matron. He didn't recognize anybody else.

He smiled at them. They didn't.

He brushed past them and walked out. He leant on the opposite wall and looked through the glass panels.

The nurse was taking out her tubes!

"NO!" He rushed inside. "Don't take out those. She might need them!"

The aged man came to him. "I'm sorry. She's no more. She had gone into a coma since yesterday…"

"But she opened her eyes just now. She shook her head… She held my hand…"

The man looked at him blankly. Then patted his back and went off. *He didn't believe him!*

He looked at her. All the tubes were taken off. Tuli sunk lifelessly into the bed. Was she dead? Did he imagine all that? *Was he going mad?*

In a trance he walked towards her. He held her hand. They were cooler than normal temperature.

"Tuli?" he called out softly. "Tuli, open your eyes. You are fine. Come on. Where's Aakash? Tuli, you promised me Aakash…" He felt a hand pull him away. *No!* He didn't want to leave her…she might stir again…

Soumen turned him around. "Let's go Neilu. It's all over."

He walked back with him in a trance. He made him sit down on a chair outside. Neil saw a barrage of people outside. They were all crying. He didn't recognize any of them. He felt sad. Someone in their family must have passed away.

He felt he was not there at all… Was he dead too?

"…viral hepatitis… one doesn't survive…" he heard voices say. "…it's horrible for Soumen… they even save the baby couldn't… his first son… extracted the fetus, yet could not save her… too much* bleeding..." He saw a woman wail and drop down on the floor. It was Tuli's mother.

Tuli was being carried away on a stretcher!

How many hours had passed? They were dressing Tuli in a bride's outfit. Pouring sindoor[38] *over her forehead. She was looking sallow but beautiful...*

Someone held his hand. He turned and saw his mother. She held his arm and sniffed. "She was so sweet...she enlivened my home... Soumen... can he take the shock?"

He freed his arm. Of course this was not happening to him. Neil smiled at his mother. He was in Remo's flat and it'd soon be daybreak. He'd take the first flight to Calcutta...

They were smearing alta on her feet. They had picked up a wooden bed she was lying on, on their shoulders...Dada was crying...

He wanted to wake up. But he found Mahamaya pulling him towards that bed. "Hold her bed," she told him.

He held it mechanically. And everyone started walking.

Neil walked for eternity. What time was it? Six in the morning? He'd be late for his flight. He looked at his watch. 4:30. p.m.? What was all this? How could it be evening? It had to be morning...

The crowd reached the burning *ghat* [38]. They had to wait in a queue. Death was lined up. There was a boy of about six bedecked in flowers. An old woman in white lay in a bed beside him. A young man was being carried off in a canvass. He had had an accident, someone said, and the canvass was a well of blood. It was his turn to enter the giant electric chamber...

The giant chamber's mouth opened and some expert hands, unhesitant and talking casually, pushed in the iron tray with the man inside on it. *The monstrous, roasting hell burning at the maximum temperature was the road to heaven!*

They had once talked about this electric chamber in college. It's said that the heat is so high that a human body took a few minutes to burn to bones. And when they took out the tray, the ashes remained on it in a human form!

Tuli's ashes would be in Tuli's form! Neil suddenly felt scared. *The gargantuan jaw was going to swallow Tuli, too!*

CHAPTER 19

He was running! He was out in the deadly night and was running! He was panting! He wanted to stop. To fall down. But he couldn't …

He opened his eyes. A very familiar ceiling with a fan spinning above came into view. Where was he? In Remo's flat? In his room? Or in their new flat?

Chot-kakima's face came into view.

"How are you?"

He looked at her blank. What was she doing in Mumbai? Where is Tuli?

He sat up. An instant sweep of blackness clouded over him and he fell back onto the pillow.

His aunt, Sharada, held his hand. "Sleep Neilu, you are too weak to get up."

"What… What happened to…?" he wanted to say Tuli, but rephrased it the last second, "…to me?"

Sharada stroked his hair, "You shouldn't have gone to the burning *ghat*. You have a weak structure…"

Burning *ghat*? "Why?" he asked.

Sharada looked at him blank. "What do you mean, 'why'?"

"Why… burning *ghat*?"

"Tuli…" she started to say and then stopped. "Sleep. I'll call *Boudi*."

His mind went blank.

Once outside, Sharada ran to Mahamaya. "I tell you, call a doctor. He doesn't seem well."

"He's in shock," said Satyendra, Neil's elder uncle, standing at the corridor, leaning against the balcony railings.

Mahamaya looked at them. Did they know? Do they all know? I hope they'll all forgive Neil.

She emphatically said, "Somu hasn't recovered either. He's lying in his room. He'd cried a lot. After all, he loved her too much."

She *had* to say that. She was holding the family's reputation in her hands. Despite her grief of losing her only *bouma* and grandson, she couldn't let one weak moment overcome her.

"He was always very sensitive and physically weak," Sharada was saying. "Why did you let him go to the burning *ghat*?"

Satyendra added, "It was terrible. Even I couldn't bear it. Ooff! Neilu just stood and fainted!"

"He needs to cry," said Sharada and the other two nodded.

Soumen was in a state of shock, too. He had to give the dead baby to the *Dom*[40], for him to bury him. He felt like crying. But something at the back of his mind said that it was *not* his baby. The doctor had said the conception was sometime towards the end of August. They hadn't gone to bed after July!

He hated the lifeless bundle as he handed it and was glad it was over.

CHAPTER 20

Calcutta, May 8 1995

The incense was very strong. At least a dozen sticks were burning simultaneously. Tuli's smiling photo that was clicked in Digha was enlarged. The frame was adorned with a big white-lily garland and *chandan* [41]. She was smiling — laughing almost. *She couldn't be.* She was so sad leaving him. Maybe she *was*. She had his son with him.

Tuli was dead. Tuli had died. She had viral hepatitis that led to fulminating viral hepatitis, leading to coma and then hepatitis failure. The baby died inside from asphyxia, or suffocation, and was extracted a day before she went into coma. It happened very quickly. Within a week. She bled profusely. She had slipped into coma the night before Neil came, even before the doctors could react timely. He had imagined all that — Tuli opening her eyes… holding her hand…

She died. His Tuli was dead. Neil told himself in all possible ways. Clinically, emotionally, logically. He understood. But there were no feelings. He was dressed in white and sat on the *thakurdalan* looking at the photograph.

The priest chanted hymns and Soumen, clad in a dhoti and a shawl, repeated them with his hands folded. Everyone sat scattered around. Everyone. There were no more place to sit and some stood with their hands folded. Digambar Roy was at the terrace — looking after his guests.

Mahamaya wiped her eyes incessantly. She felt she had dominated the little girl too much. *If only she was married to Neil…*

Soumen looked at the smiling face and felt guilty. Maybe, he really didn't try to get to know her. Maybe, he really never cared and truly never loved her. Maybe he never saw beyond a wild night of sex with her. He remembered her breasts. They were wonderful. Her figure was wonderful. How could he have stayed away? And anyway, he never had the time to stop and think what she really wanted. Probably she had an affair with Neil. He understood her. And forgave her.

Sharada nudged at Sonali, Neil's older aunt, "I knew it all along. I saw her coming down the stairs so many times. Look at Neil's face, look, look."

Sonali smiled, "*Boudi* is trying to cover it up. But who knows whose baby she was carrying?"

Satyendra and Surendra stood attending the guests. They really felt sad. Somehow the girl had stolen their hearts. She was so lively. Surendra wiped his eyes often.

Sujoy looked at his *boudi*'s photograph and silently shed tears. Neepa saw that and hugged her brother. Rumpa and Chompa played upstairs with their maid.

Dr Bhattacharya stood at one corner. He had come a while back and would leave immediately. He folded his hands and looked at the picture. What a lively face! Why are doctors still helpless in the hands of fate? Why couldn't she live? She had a whole world bursting in colored rhododendrons for her. Why did she have to die? He had not seen many miracles in his life. But when he was examining her lifeless eyes, his fingers *had* felt wet. He realized Neil wasn't lying or imagining things. Tuli *had* cried just before dying. *Maybe she had opened her eyes!*

Neil felt alienated from everything. He felt he was not there. He was thinking of Hassan. He had to speak to his travel agent today. He looked at his watch. It was 11 a.m. He stood up and left the house. He was planning to catch a flight that evening…

Mahamaya looked at her younger son leaving. *She knew she was losing him forever….*

IBRAHIM HASSAN

CHAPTER 1

Mumbai, June 24 1995

It had been a hot day. Vikram Bhatt was sweating despite his AC BMW. The traffic was incessant. He had to reach Nariman Towers at 7.00 p.m.

"Pull the car, fast," he ordered his chauffer.

"Yes, sir.

The car swung onto Holker Chowk from Karve Road and then turned right onto Marine Drive. The sea looked good. Bhatt was tempted to pull down the power windows and feel some of the breeze. His wife had told him often to reduce some of the fat. How he wished he wasn't so heavy and sweaty. He paid thousands on girls, but he never seemed to make them happy. Anyway, this was no time to think of girls. He had a date with Juhi that night. She was getting too inquisitive and pricey. He knew she belonged to Barry. He knew Barry's kingdom knew no bounds. But he was no small taker. He had the support of Hassan*bhai* and D'Souza.

Juhi was also getting friendly with this new boy Hassan hired. The boy is good. From what he heard, this boy was becoming a Remo's right-hand man. Bengalis were soft-hearted. He knew that.

He had a Bengali friend long ago. But this Bengali was a real tiger. He'd soon make it big, Bhatt felt.

The BMW swung into Nariman Towers. The forty-two-storey building looked enticing. Here the 52-year-old business tycoon was to enter into a new consignment deal with Hassan. This time it would involve the Indian Customs. He would have to import arms from the Middle East. But he was prepared for it. Things were going great guns for him.

He had an official business of transportation and of importing dry fruits from a neighboring country. In the past twenty-six years he had never felt better. He had connections with Hassan, the lord of all times and nothing could pin him down.

He stepped out of the car heavily as his chauffer opened the door for him. He hated to take the lift. He hated the smell of his sweat to get enclosed in such a small chamber. He had tried out all imported after-shaves, but with little result. He had to go for a treatment. But he wasn't finding the time.

But now he would have more time on his hands. This deal with Hassan*bhai* was going to make him a shade richer than the mafia boss himself. But that was unofficial. He would buy an island in the Maldives and build a dream domain there. He owed that to his wife. She had seen him through his good and bad times.

Then he would dump Hassan.

In fact, he was already thinking of operating from the Maldives. He would have to, after he signed another deal with Joseph D'Souza, Hassan's stark enemy. D'Souza had offered him a sumptuous deal for dumping Hassan. He had agreed. The Goanese was smaller in power compared to Hassan, but D'Souza was a pet of Police Commissioner, Prakash Bhalla.

Then Bhatt could talk. He felt cheeky. Bhatt held a lot of secrets of Ibrahim Hassan's empire. He remembered the times Hassan threw him out of his house for sleeping around with his mistress. He never forgot a hurt in a hurry. Every dog had his day. He was waiting for the day when Hassan would come begging at his feet.

He had two mafia bosses eating out of his hands. He felt powerful and wanted.

The lift reached the 42nd floor. The door opened and an electronic voice said, "Welcome to Café de Santana". The lift led opened into the café.

Bhatt walked out. A part of the terrace was converted into a café under a dome-shaped brown glass ceiling. Concealed lights, music and lots of greenery set a warm arena. The upholstery was in green and brown that complemented the ambiance.

There were very few people around. A couple in their mid-thirties sat holding hands, a family of four, and two men, sitting and talking business. He spotted Remo. Remo was signing the deals nowadays. He was sitting at a table near the door leading out to the terrace, with that Bengali guy. He waved at him. Remo waved back.

"Hi, how are you?" Vikram Bhatt extended his hand.

"Fine. This is Neil."

"Hello."

"Hello," said Neil.

"I have very little time," said Bhatt after sitting down heavily onto the chair. The chair was too small. His large bottom hung out from two ends of the chair.

"Relax. Where's the hurry?" Remo said calmly.

"No," he smiled, "I have an appointment at eight."

"Huh, huh!" sneered Remo sipping on his coffee, "Girlfriend?"

Bhatt smiled. Did Remo know he had an appointment with his girlfriend, Juhi?

"Let's get down to business," Bhatt insisted. "Do you have the papers?"

"Yes. Neil, show him the papers."

Neil took out a set of documents from his bag. They were contract documents. Contracts for shipment of cars from Dubai. That was official. In reality, it was shipment of arms hidden inside the bonnets. Bhatt went through the papers thoroughly. He was happy with the deal.

"Good, everything is in order. Where do I sign?"

Remo and Neil glanced at each other. "Here," he pointed out.

Bhatt scribbled his signature. Remo took the document.

"I don't have a copy. Er… can I send it to you tomorrow?"

Bhatt was a little disappointed. Remo was an ace player. He could not have made such a mistake. "Alright," he smiled. "We know each other for years now."

"Yeah!" Remo suddenly stood up. "Let's celebrate!"

"Not today. Today I …"

"…Have an appointment with Juhi, right?"

Bhatt was flustered. That bitch! She was playing games with him!

"No, I mean…"

"Come outside. Let's have a smoke. The terrace looks so calm."

Both Remo and Neil goaded him on to the terrace. Bhatt decided to go along. He hadn't much choice.

The terrace was a well-chosen spot. It had a soft breeze blowing, a starry night above and *no boundary walls*.

Remo led him to a dark spot. Neil followed from behind.

"Look, it's so peaceful. You need these types of breaks, Bhatt."

"Yah, I know," Bhatt was clearly impressed. It had been a long time since he had relaxed.

"You can weigh your situation better when you are out amidst nature," Remo turned and was explaining.

"Yah," Bhatt inhaled fresh air.

"Like why you should dump Hassan and join D'Souza!"

"What?!" Bhatt thought he had heard wrong.

"You heard me." Remo's voice was of steel.

"What are you speaking about? Why should I dump Hassan? And who's this D'Souza?" He looked behind him. They had come around to the back of the café where nobody could see them. Neil smoked a cigarette with one hand in his pocket, standing behind him. He wouldn't be able to escape or scream for help. Music was blaring inside.

"Let me refresh your memory." Remo begun, "D'Souza is Hassan's strongest enemy but…" his voice became a whisper, "his greatest friend personally. They had both started together. *Not* knowing this was your biggest mistake."

"I… I…" Bhatt stuttered.

"And about dumping Hassan… You know, I have instructions to throw you *live* off the terrace?"

Bhatt couldn't believe this was happening to him. His face ran out of all color!

"But I'll spare you that anxiety... I'll first shoot you and then throw you down."

Bhatt looked at Remo's hand unbelievably. He had an automatic pointed at him.

"Remo... Remo... I'll pay you double...triple... five times of what Hassan paid you. And who told you I was joining D'Souza? I am fine here." He realized he had reached the end of the terrace.

"Please Remo, I have a wife and two children..."

"Sorry, Vikram. I took a lot of money for this."

The first bullet struck him below his stomach. The second his chest. There were no sounds. *I guess he's fitted a silencer, Bhatt thought.* And then he saw Remo lifting him into air...

When Neil and Remo came out on the streets, there was a small crowd around Bhatt's body drowned in blood. They gulped canned Pepsi, which they had bought from the café while coming down, and walked towards their white Cielo. They stepped inside; the driver started the car and zoomed off, passing by a stream of police vehicles screaming with sirens.

CHAPTER 2

Mumbai, May 11 1995

Hassan was confused.

He had dealt with many young men in the ten years of his profession. He liked the enthusiastic staff. He was aging. He could hand over Remo Gujjar his kingdom after he left. His life was under constant threat. Though no major crime was directly committed by him and the commissioners were easy to buy out, he feared the Central Bureau of Investigations, the CBI. A tiny mistake, and he could face the worst.

He had trained Remo likewise. To take over if anything happened to him. But this new friend of his confused him. He had good blood, he presumed. And had a fire of a king in his eyes. Hassan had never before liked anybody else like this. He always preferred logic. Logically, this boy would take a long time to become professional. He just couldn't do things that he thought were wrong. And he thought what Hassan did was wrong. This was the first time somebody *refused* to be associated with him. Refused lakhs of rupees.

Hassan saw through those eyes at their first meeting. He was an inborn prince, a future king.

The aged man stood on the white semi circular balcony that had ornate cement boundary walls, overlooking his blue swimming pool and then the Arabian Sea.

He was in a white *churidar-kurta* and was watching the sunset. This was one private moment he vied for, to be alone with himself, every day. Not that he always got the opportunity. Today he had.

He weighed his standing in life. His two sons were grown up and were tilling land back in his village in Purnia, in Bihar. They hadn't a clue what their father had been up to during the last ten years. Not that they cared too much. They were happy with the money that he sent them. He too hadn't seen them for a long time. He never missed his children much. He never ever had felt a fatherly instinct — until *now!*

Remo told him about Neil's involvement with his sister-in-law and the baby. He also had stated Neil's dislike for taking any obligations from him. That piqued his curiosity and he wanted to meet the boy. He usually never offered his aircraft to all. But something in Neil's eyes made him do that. A sadness, a fire, an intense passion, a fanatical courage — all which he thought his heir should possess. It required no mean intensity and valor to be involved with one's sister-in-law, accept his baby within her and then decide to marry her. He was impressed with the unimposing yet unassailable quality that he projected.

And a while back, Remo informed him over the phone about the terrible mishap.

He was thinking. He was revaluing his decision.

His cell phone chimed out a latest chartbuster. He walked over and picked it up from the cane table.

It was Halim. "Yes?"

"*Bhai*, Bhatt has agreed to the deal with D'souza."

Hassan felt a blocked emotion. The kind of emotion he felt whenever he felt cheated. His jaws tightened. "I'll speak to D'Souza."

"Sir?" Asif was at the door. He turned and switched off the phone.

"That new *saab* has come."

"New...?" Then he realized. "Send him in."

Neil was in a pair of jeans and a yellow T-shirt. His face was expressionless. His eyes were cold.

"Come in, come in, my son!" Hassan's warmth was spontaneous. He put his arms around the boy. "I've heard everything. Please consider this your home. We are all with you."

He made Neil sit down on the sofa. "What would you like? Scotch? Smirnoff?" Neil looked up at him with vacant eyes. Hassan ordered to Asif, "Serve us Scotch."

Asif did the needful. He poured the golden liquid into two exclusive looking tumblers. He filled up the tumblers with ice cubes.

Hassan waved his hand. Asif understood. He left, closing the door behind him.

"Don't let anybody in," he instructed the armed guard sitting on a stool outside the room.

Hassan handed the glass to Neil, "Here, relax yourself."

Neil took the glass mechanically. He sipped on the liquid and felt better. He decided to speak. He didn't want to waste any more of Hassan's time.

"I want to… join you," he framed his intentions.

Hassan looked at him surprised. Then resumed composure. "Good." He was tempted to ask why he had changed his mind, but refrained from it.

He asked, "Right away?"

Neil nodded.

"Fine. You start by learning the business. Remo knows how to go about with the collections. He has the organizations listed. Don't hesitate to follow his commands. And don't shoot at anybody now. I'll give you orders for that. I'll give you an advance of a lakh for your personal expenses. This is just to begin with. Once you can operate on your own and learn the tricks of the trade, I'll increase the amount."

Neil listened to him, astounded!

Hassan smiled: "A lakh of rupees is nothing. Considering the kind of risks you'll be taking…" He stopped.

Then thinking something he added, "You're not scared, are you?"

Neil looked up. The blaze in his eyes said it all. Even then he spoke. This time the inferno in his voice made Hassan feel relaxed.

"I have no hang-ups about my life. But it's my loyalty and gratitude to you that I want you to understand."

"I do." Hassan put in quickly. He did. Neil sighed and gulped down the liquid.

Hassan leant back onto the sofa and said, "Will you feel better if you tell me your pain?"

"No." Neil was curt. He looked down at his emptying glass. Hassan felt a jolt. But he liked it. Nobody ever refused him flat on his face. This boy has all the qualities. He was tempted to tell him what he had in mind. But he knew he'd be impulsive.

"It's all right then..." he walked out of the room into his bedroom. Neil finished the liquid fast. Hassan came out with a black pouch with a leather handle — the kinds a clerk in Calcutta would carry rushing to office with his tiffin box in it. He handed it to Neil. Neil looked at it. *A hundred thousand rupees in it?!*

"I had bought this pouch at Bandra Station with my first money. I thought I'd carry my tiffin box in it. I used to be very hungry in those days." Hassan smiled and the gold tooth sparkled. "Now I barely eat."

He paused. Neil thought he saw a sparkle of water in his eyes. He took the pouch. "Don't lose it. This'll bring you good luck."

Neil looked at the pouch and then at the man. He felt a pang. His own pain seemed lesser. He walked slowly out.

Hassan picked up the phone a while later and dialed.

"D'Souza?"

"Hassan! What a lucky day! What made you call?"

"I want to talk to you about Vikram Bhatt."

CHAPTER 3

Versova, Mumbai, October 19 1995

"Hey both of you, go to sleep." Remo said, putting his feet up on the sofa handle. He closed his eyes. It was apparent that the marijuana had got to him. Neil was fine. He took another puff and put his feet up on the centre table. He nudged at Juhi who was leaning on him.

"Hmm…" Juhi mumbled.

"Juhi, Juhi, let's go outside," Neil said.

She sat up. With difficulty she opened her eyes. "Where?" She said groggily.

"Let's go to the beach."

"You're mad! It must be past two." she said and put her head back onto Neil's shoulder.

Neil decided he wanted to go. He tried to get up. Juhi held him down. "I want to make love to you, Neil, please, let's go inside…"

Neil got up. Juhi fell straight on the sofa. He bent and patted her cheeks.

He locked the door behind him and walked out. It was extremely dangerous for him to step out right now. Hassan*bhai* had repeatedly told them not to step out of the bungalow. They were supposed to be very careful. Though he had a sitting with the commissioner and offered Bhalla two crores of rupees to drop the case, the honest commissioner was yet to be bought.

It had been over a month that they were confined to Hassan's bungalow in Madh Island. Matters seemed to be dying a natural death. But Hassan said nothing could be trusted unless Bhalla officially closed the case. Neil and Remo were shifted in disguise and separately in different cars at different locations for the past four months. It had been a trying period. Neil was fed up with the hide-and-seek and wanted to flee. But Hassan wasn't the type one could play games with. Juhi visited them every day. She wasn't supposed to. But she was hopelessly in love with Neil and didn't care.

Neil stepped out into the fresh air. The two armed guards Hassan assigned for them were asleep in sitting positions. Neil was thankful. They would not have let him out.

The bungalow was on a deserted stretch facing the raging Arabian Sea. It led out into a garden. The iron gates of the bungalow were locked. He took out the keys from his pocket and undid the lock stealthily. Then he softly opened one black gate and squeezed outside, closing the gate, unlocked, after him.

The wide road he stepped onto was void of any life. It was illuminated by brilliant yellow sodium vapor lights hanging atop lofty posts. Beyond that, a part of the gigantic expanse of the rocky beach had turned orange with the illumination. Ahead of that — everything was dark, sinister, eclipsed.

Neil felt a trifle scared. He felt his pocket for his automatic and felt better.

He walked towards the beach. A rocky boulevard welcomed him. His feet felt through the jutting rocks and slipped often. This was an abandoned part of the beach which nobody really explored. It was dark, and yet with a determination edging towards self-destruction, Neil scampered over the boulders to reach his destination. He could hear the sea calling him. Inviting him to run away from his life. After a precarious walk of over almost half a mile over cruel rocks, he stepped off onto soft sands. His feet sank into them. Then he saw the sea. Raging and wild.

There was no moon in the sky. Stars were sprinkled thickly on the black canvas… as if the entire galaxy had come down to watch the earth. He felt the breeze lifting him off into the air. The water shone brightly with phosphorous. It raved like a caged animal beating against the sand with vengeance.

He sat down on the sand near the water. The waves were crawling up to his feet and crawling back. He waited for a giant wave. He wouldn't move. He would get wet.

The ocean swayed in front of him. He didn't like it. He never liked getting inebriated. Yet he was getting more and more hooked on to this intoxication.

He asked himself. Why? What was he escaping from? Himself? His pain? So many people love him. So many... his father, his mother, Sujoy, Neepa, Juhi, Remo, Hassan... So many people. One barely gets this kind of love in a lifetime.

Love? Love him? Really? All these people love him? Will they love him if they knew that he was a *criminal* — in every form?

He threw back his head into the sand. He lay flat and looked up to the sky. Criminal. Yes. A *chosen profession*. He held his head and closed his eyes. He felt he was sinking into the sand. He wanted to open his eyes. He couldn't.

He could have continued with his job. A well-paid, secured job, where Sonia was ever ready to be his wife. He could wipe out the entire existence he had lived for so long and started life afresh. Of course, Juhi would have been angry. But she was a friend. He could explain that to her. How important her friendship was to him, than her being his wife.

So why did he throw it all up?

Because he's a criminal. He *loved* to be a criminal. He loved to move against the tide and be an anti-social.

Was he in love with Tuli? Or was he in love with her *being in love with him*? If he did love her, why did he escape her death? Why did he run away? If he didn't love her *why did he have an affair with his brother's wife?* Why did he make her pregnant? *Why did he push her to her death...?*

Because he's a *criminal*. He's a born criminal.

He hit his hand very hard on the sand and turned to his side. He loved Juhi. How could he? How *could* he love anybody again?

He turned over again and opened his eyes. The stars seemed to be crowding down upon him. They all seemed to hate him. Everyone. The sky, the stars, the raging sea...

Because now he's a criminal. A *legal* one. A branded activist in Hassan's gang. Within a year he had become the most coveted man for the Mumbai police. He was fleeing from the law. Why was he always fleeing? Why was he escaping? Why couldn't he anchor somewhere? Why couldn't he make *someone* happy?

He turned to the other side. And then he spotted her.

TULI!

She was in a sari and jumping to and fro with the waves. He opened his eyes. She was gone!

What was that?! Did he imagine her with his eyes closed? Did he see her? Tuli *was* here. So lively. So lovely. Why didn't God give him Tuli? God was bad. He was terrible. If he had Tuli he would have never let her go. He would have had a different life altogether. *His son!* He's gone too. He must hate his father. A coward father. A criminal father.

Tuli won't hate him. *Will she?* Maybe she did. Maybe she didn't show it. *But I loved her…* I really did… He clutched a handful of sand as his only support. It slipped out. He became very angry and clutched onto it again. It slipped out again. He started beating on the sand. His fist made a small crater. He didn't care. *I loved her… I loved her… Yes! I really did…*

"*…Why did she leave me….!!!*" He wailed out! He threw his hands into the air and screamed at the black sky. The wail came in a gasp and he screamed again, "I am not a criminal… I wanted to live life like a normal human being…" He stood up suddenly and began running into the water. His pants became thick with sand and water and his legs felt heavy. But he moved… With all his strength he moved into knee-deep water. And then fell down and sobbed. "I am *not* a criminal… I am a good person… I want to live life normally… *I want to…*" He wailed and sobbed. And sat down in the sea. The waves raged over his head, as if punishing him for everything, not heeding a word of what he was saying. He didn't care… the salt water was seeping into his mouth… He gulped it and tried to throw it out. He felt he was being swept into the current. He liked it. He wanted to die… to reach Tuli.

She'd laugh at him and tell him, "How can you think like that? You are such a sweetheart. *The most loveable person on earth…*"

And then he knew it!

He escaped from Tuli's death because his own pain was unbearable. He became numb with pain, with blocking up every frenzied emotion he felt at that juncture. He would have become hysterical if he had let *one* tear drop.

He escaped from Sonia's clutches because he never wanted to love anybody else. He barely liked her and didn't want to build his whole life on this faint emotion. It would have been a house of cards. He didn't want to gamble. He didn't love Juhi but took her as a friend. And can't hurt her. So to keep her happy he played being in love. Of course, he enjoyed sex with her. That was the second phase of his self-destruction. He was using Juhi to destroy himself and reinstate the aura of the word 'love' in a junk form so he forgot Tuli faster. He forgot his pain sooner.

His first act of self-destruction was when he had decided to join Hassan. He wanted to walk on the edge of life. He suddenly felt he had not taken life by the neck when it was needed. And when he decided to do so, life simply slipped out of his hands. Now he wanted to throw life up into the air — simply walk towards death. There was nothing for him to live on. He wanted to join Tuli fast. *Come fast...* she had said. *She was waiting for him.*

The immense loss of self-esteem that he encountered for a few minutes was restored. The oscillation of his existence — from being a boy brought up under Indian ethics and surrounded by superstitions, very conservatively Bengali, to a youth believing in his own logic and lifestyle — stopped. He had already led a life set by his own norms for a long time and he couldn't today turn to his roots for support. His roots wouldn't support him anyway. He never believed in them. He couldn't have the fill of two worlds. He had found hard reality. He couldn't move backwards.

His muscles relaxed and he felt the sea pulling him inside her womb...

The police found him at 4:30 a.m. lying face down on an abandoned part of Madh Island beach. They first thought he was dead. Then realizing that he wasn't, Inspector Shinde gave orders for him to be transferred to the city government hospital. Shinde was a very happy man. He had arrested both the prime suspects of the Vikram Bhatt murder case.

Remo was arrested from Hassan's bungalow with a call girl and had already been deported to the lock up. They had thought Neil had got away. Escaped. But, Shinde felt proud of his instincts. He decided to comb-search the beach. Since the man didn't have a vehicle, he couldn't have gone far on foot. His instincts proved correct. His men didn't have to go very far.

He wound the baton around his fingers and smiled at the dawn breaking on the ocean. He was going to speak about a promotion to Bhalla.

CHAPTER 4

Bombay Central Jail, September 17 1996

Neil stared at the gray ceiling. The sky outside the small vent high up on the wall, shone brightly. It must be a sunny day outside. No one discerned it from this cell, so cut off from civilization.

He didn't care. A year of confinement in this cell, away from reality had made all his senses grow numb. He liked it. He liked the numbness that was growing within him. He liked the way the police were treating him. He liked the second-degree tortures. His bones had been broken near his elbow and jaw and mended without any treatment, over the period.

Despite Hassan's repeated instructions to Shinde of not touching him or Remo physically, Shinde had a wonderful time spending his off hours with them. He even enjoyed sex with them. Neil began to enjoy the hours with him too. Those were his moments of penance. The case was going on for a year and they were not given bail, despite Hassan's desperate attempts. They were kept in solitary cells and treated like animals.

The case would be over today. Today was the day of judgment. Neil knew what the judgment would be. So much had Hassan's lawyer fed him with the slanted details that he was beginning to forget what really happened. Neil knew Hassan was trying to help him out.

But he knew the mafia man was trying to corner Remo. The entire cause for the mishap was getting slowly shifted onto Remo's

185

shoulders as the case proceeded. He felt bad for Remo. The boy had set a lot of hope on Hassan. But he had a series of extortion rackets and six murders in his books. Even God couldn't come and help him out.

The only bright aspect of the case was that there were no witnesses to the murders he committed. He had been careful about that and Neil did not give him away. Even then, as the case proceeded Remo realized he was being slowly pushed against the wall. Remo became a bitter and broken man.

"Cheer up," Neil had whispered to him the last day they crossed each other at the courtroom. "Things are going to go in our favor."

Remo looked at him vacantly. "Things are going in *your* favor."

Neil was tempted to ask him, "Why?" but restrained himself. He wondered why Hassan was trying to pull him out of the case. He didn't believe the big man would actually betray Remo. When Hassan came to meet him a week ago Neil had asked him directly. "Why are you letting down Remo?"

Hassan had looked at him sadly. "That's not your business," he said calmly. He didn't add, *Remo's becoming very powerful, an emergent threat. I want to put him off for a few years.* He didn't add, *'It's for you, son'.*

Neil postponed the discussion. He was going to find out after he came out.

The hearing the last day went completely in his favor.

"And so M'Lord," Atul Bakshi was summing up. "My client Remo Gujjar was pushed into firing in an act of defending his friend as Vikram Bhatt tried to push Neil overboard. As I told you repeatedly, it was a minor quarrel; about Remo not getting the copy of the contract they signed that day. My exhibits, of the contract signed by him, are with you. They were standing out in the terrace and talking casually. He was offering Remo a lot of money to buy him off. When he refused, Bhatt got abusive. Neil tried to calm him and Bhatt tried to push him overboard. It was then Remo took out his gun in an act of protecting his friend. Remo had no intentions of shooting. The gun accidentally took off in the tussle, two bullets hit him and Bhatt fell off the terrace, not being able to withstand the impact. The case is an open and shut one, M'lord."

The 49-year-old lawyer had not a scrap of regret in his voice. Bhatt had cheated out on his brother long time back and made him hang himself. He thought Bhatt deserved to die. And to top it all, Rs 50 lakhs were in his pocket. Hassan had promised him another fifty, if he handled the case the way Hassan wanted him to.

The opposition lawyer was junior to Bakshi and was fed with Rs 10 lakhs for sinking the case. His defense was therefore meek and not supported by any witnesses. Bhatt didn't have a high-ranking mafia man in his support. His widowed wife was fighting the case alone. And she knew she had lost it even before it had started. She had two small children. She didn't want to lose them. It was as though Bakshi was the judge and was passing the verdict himself.

Though Bakshi clubbed Neil and Remo into the act and even haloed Remo's action as that of a loyal friend trying to save Neil's life, he had essentially cornered Remo. The gun was always in Remo's hand and Neil was the innocent man caught up in the act.

Neil knew what would be the verdict today. He would be a free man and Remo would serve the minimum imprisonment. For the kind of act they should have both been *sentenced to death*.

He thought about Sujoy and Neepa. Of Rumpa and Chompa. Of his mother and father. He had sent them only a few letters during the past year through Asif and had asked him to post it from a convenient location.

He thought of the gigantic mouth of the burning electric chamber that had swallowed Tuli. He thought about the small lifeless bundle he hadn't seen. Aakash must have looked like him. He felt nauseated and went to a corner where the commode was kept, to vomit…

Remo sat in his bunk reading the day's newspaper with one eye. His other eye was pierced through by Shinde. He felt a peace within him. A painless happiness. He knew what the verdict was going to be today. He wasn't angry with Neil. The boy never gave him away even through the most harrowing of tortures. He wasn't angry with Hassan either. He knew Neil was being used as a pawn to remove him. He was simply angry with himself. For trusting Hassan like he would trust his father. He had kept his hope alive till the last minute. But now that was blown off, he felt a peace within himself. He also realized he'd never go back to Hassan. After serving his time, he'd go back to Calcutta and start a business of his own. He thought of his mother, his heavy-bosomed mother and started to cry…

Hassan, Bakshi and Bhalla were seated at Hassan's mansion in Pali Hill. They raised their glasses in the air together. "Cheers!" they said.

CATHY AND HODOLCHUA

CHAPTER 1

Bhuntar, Himalayas, Oct 9 1996 6:30 p.m.

"So what did you do after you were freed by the police?" Cathy asked.

They were sitting huddled on the floor of the balcony of the hotel, facing the mountains. Neil leant back on the wall and threw his burnt out cigarette out of the railings. The evening was fading out and the pink colored snow-peaks were turning a bluish white hue bathing in the glow of the moon. The chill was getting heavier.

"I went to Remo's flat and took out my stuff and went to the new flat which Hassan had rented for me at Versova, kept my things and then met Hassan."

"It seems like he likes you very much."

"Yah, as long as I danced to his tune."

"What did he say?" Cathy asked.

Neil's mind wandered off. He was planning an escape. As escape from Hassan.

"Hello?" Cathy waved a hand in front of his eyes.

"Huh…?" Neil smiled. And sighed. Then looked down and said, "Hassan hugged me and asked me to resume my work immediately."

"And what did you say?"

"I said I needed a break and would like to visit the mountains. He said, he'd pay for it. I refused."

"You don't look like you're going to join back Hassan."

"I don't know. I might have to, considering the kind of money he spent on releasing me…" He looked away. He was still thinking of an escape. Escaping into a land where Hassan or his men would not be able to find him.

Cathy suddenly smiled, "And what about the 20 women you said you had slept with? When did you do that?"

"Oh!" Neil laughed. "I was pulling your leg. Yah, I became quite a womanizer after Tuli's death — going to brothels and spending nights with call girls. I was heavily into extortion rackets and was becoming a morbid man."

"What about Juhi? What did you tell her?"

"Nothing. I never committed myself to her. She had a nice heart. I enjoyed sex with her." He smiled at Cathy.

She cast her eyes down. "Hmm…" she said philosophically.

Then she looked up. "When did you last speak about these things to anyone?"

Neil was taken aback. He looked at the mountains. "I've never spoken about myself before."

"Then why are you telling me?" she asked.

He looked at her deeply. Then looked down. "I don't know. I thought you could be trusted…"

Then he looked away and shrugged. "Maybe you'll go away and my secret will go with you… Maybe it's the mountains… maybe," he looked at her, slightly bewildered, "Maybe I am falling in love with you."

Cathy laughed and leant forward to hold his hand, "Neil, you'll never love anybody again."

He looked away. He let her hold his hand. The intoxicating evening, the blue mountains and the camouflage of the dimly lit, silent balcony made him shiver. He didn't want to fall in love again.

He sighed, "I think I like you very much." He clasped her hand in his and looked into her eyes. "I think we can start off as friends."

Cathy smiled and looked down, "Yeah sure." Then looked up, "Only I don't know what I am going to explain to Mike."

"Mike?"

"My husband." They realized they hadn't spoken about him at all. Neil felt a familiar guilt. He freed his hand.

"No Cathy, I am not getting involved with another married woman. It's too costly an affair."

"But I thought we'd be friends."

Neil looked at her with the corner of his eyes and smiled mischievously, "I don't like the look in your eyes."

They both laughed. Cathy leant forward and kissed him on his cheeks on an impulse. Then she became serious and planted a light kiss on his lips. Neil kept looking at her. She raised a finger and ran it down his forehead, nose and lips — down his throat. He gulped and closed his eyes. They let the hunger grow and Cathy shifted close. Neil placed his lips on her and spoke against them, "We shouldn't..."

Cathy whispered, "I know..."

They kissed, lightly at first, then passionately. Neil pulled Cathy on his lap and they kissed for, what seemed, years. Cathy pulled out for breath and said, "We should go down and eat. We haven't eaten anything since breakfast."

Neil ran his finger lightly down her neck, up her breasts, down her stomach and legs, "Yes, what should we have for dinner?"

Cathy buried her face in his stomach, "Leech," she said.

Neil smiled and ran his finger up her buttocks and her back, "Yes, with tomato sauce."

Cathy nodded and held him around his waist, "I'd like mine fried."

"Good," Neil said and clasped her hair to turn her face, "But first we must have an appetizer. Your room or mine?"

CHAPTER 2

Towards Pulga, October 10 1996

"Ambik had asked to look out for the last step," Neil said, panting.

"Who's Ambik??" Cathy asked after catching up.

"He was a friend in college." He panted for some more breath and held out his hand for Cathy. She balanced over two boulders and clutched onto Neil's hand. Then leaped over to the small flat land Neil was standing.

"How much more?" she asked.

"Another hour."

"Let's rest,' said Cathy and flopped on a boulder beside the path. Neil took out a mineral water bottle from his rucksack and gave it to Cathy. She gulped down the slightly salty liquid, drenching her parched throat.

"I can't climb anymore," she handed him the bottle.

Neil drank his fill and stuffed the bottle back inside. "What would you have done if you hadn't met me?"

"I would have gone back," she said promptly.

"So go back, who's stopping you?" Neil zipped up his rucksack.

Cathy looked at him with crossed eyebrows, "I wished I could." And then broke into a smile.

He sat down beside her. She turned to him. "What was the village we had breakfast in?"

"Oonch. It's the major village here."

"What was the last step you were talking about?"

"Oh! It seems until you take the last step you wouldn't be able to see Pulga. After a tough climb, you take your last step and suddenly you see a vast green valley, filled with apple trees, surrounded by snow-capped mountains. It's a wonderful and a stunning sight, I believe."

"Oh yeah? I heard there are no hotels up there. Only log huts."

"Great! I love log huts. People take tents up there too."

"But we don't have tents. Where do we stay if we don't find an accommodation?"

"Don't worry," Neil looked at her mischievously, "If not anything, you'll sleep in my lap."

"Very funny." She smiled.

"There's a surprise for you up there," Neil raised his eyebrows.

"What?"

"You'll see."

"No, tell me."

"How will I tell you if it's a surprise?"

"Then why did you pique my curiosity? It's unfair."

"Okay, okay," he paused. "The valley also grows *charas* trees. *Charas*, you know? Hashish? It's very cheap out there."

Cathy looked at him and nodded, "Yeah, I had heard something like that too."

"And so you decided on this trek route," Neil teased.

She looked away, "I don't smoke."

"But you have to live with a smoker for another two days."

She looked down. And then turned to him, "I don't mind living with this smoker for the rest of my life."

Neil looked at her shocked! She cast her eyes down and looked at the burst of colors at the forest below them. The river Parvati, which they had to cross several times on foot just over boulders, appeared a thin ribbon now. Beyond that were mountains, colorful and snow-capped, flanking this world as if severing it completely from reality.

She spoke categorically, "You want to escape from Hassan right? I'll give you an offer. You have a passport, simply get a visa and fly down to Stockholm." She looked at him, "I'll work out something."

Neil turned serious, "Thanks, I'll remember."

Cathy held his hand, "There're no strings attached to the offer. We'll be friends as we had decided."

He smiled at her, "Yah, the kind of friends we've been since yesterday."

She smiled back, "That was all… well, I couldn't help it…" Then stopped. And turned to the forest and shrugged, "And anyway, what does it matter if we let ourselves go? We are attracted to each other. It's all a part of friendship."

Neil was thinking seriously. That would be the land where nothing could touch him anymore. No pains. No obligations. No ties. No commitment.

"Let's go," he stood up.

CHAPTER 3

New Delhi, October 14 1996

Neil stared at the ceiling. The chandelier had one bulb missing. The hotel had excellent services. A 3-star hotel with a tennis court, lawn and AC rooms. They had arrived in Delhi the day before. Cathy's flight was on the 15th, the day after. This was the last day they had in hand.

He felt a pang. He looked beside him. Cathy slept soundly. Her covers pulled up to her bare shoulders. It was almost 5 a.m. but Neil couldn't sleep. They had made love until late last night. He loved her company. He felt terrible to let her go.

He instantly thought of Tuli. His sense of loyalty made him do so. Then he postponed the thought. He didn't want to think of her. He was at the brim of starting life all over again. He didn't want anything to pull him back.

He looked at her. Her golden hair had fallen all over her face. He leant over, pushed the hair and kissed her lightly on the forehead. She stirred a little and then went back to sleep.

Neil pulled up. He was feeling uneasy.

He stepped down from the bed and lit a cigarette. Then walked over to the large glass windows and removed a part of the curtain. From the 10th storey, the world looked far away. The sun was waking up, a rotund, red ball above the horizon. He thought the sky had a red tinge, until he realized the windowpanes were tinted. The world below seemed clamorous — a thick jungle of concrete, a jungle without emotions, a jungle without love. He looked at the sky. Tuli was somewhere there. His mind told him not to think of her. But his heart continued to do so. Is there really life after death? When will she be reborn again? Will she be reborn at all? Did she attain *moksha* — the freedom of the soul? Was she somewhere around, close to him? In this room?

He quickly looked around. And then laughed at his childishness. No. He told himself. I am going to start life afresh. I am not going to let life haul me down. There's Cathy. And I want to love her, if needed, marry her. Have children. Lead a normal life in an alien land — where no conscience can follow me anymore.

He still felt uneasy.

Cathy woke up. Neil was calling her softly.

"Wake up, Ma'm... it's tea time"

"Hmm.... what's the time?"

"It's evening."

"What?" Cathy crossed her eyebrows. And then realizing he was joking, she rubbed her eyes, "Oh ho..."

Neil hugged her like a baby and pulled her up to him, "You were dreaming about Mike."

She looked at him bewildered.

"Hmm... you were saying 'I love you Mike, I don't want to go anywhere.' Neil mimicked in a groggy voice.

"What rubbish!" Cathy stroked his hair. "We have long since mentally separated."

"Then why are you staying together?" Neil asked, suddenly getting serious. He realized he wanted to know. Cathy sat up and held her head, "Pass me the tea, please."

Neil stood up and brought the tray, which the bell-boy had brought in a while back and placed it on the bed. He poured tea from the pot, added a teaspoon of sugar and extended the black tea to Cathy. By now he knew how she liked her tea.

Cathy sipped it and looked up to him. "Good tea," she said.

Neil made a cup for himself and climbed on the bed beside her. "Yes, what were you saying about Mike?"

"*I* was saying? You were asking." She said and then looked down at her tea. "We're friends. We haven't legally divorced each other because we didn't feel the urge to. We're staying under the same roof because we didn't have a reason to move away physically."

"Then?" Neil was slightly bewildered.

Cathy ruffled his hair, "Young man, you have never been married. How will you know the complicacies of a marriage?"

"I want to know." Neil was serious.

"Okay." Cathy raised her eyebrows. "See, right after marriage we realized we were not mentally compatible. We couldn't satisfy each other's emotional needs. So we moved away physically for some time. Then we realized we could be good friends, in fact, good roommates. We valued each other's opinions in our personal matters as long as there were no expectations. We led our own lives. We met at dinner table just as two roommates would and shared jokes and events of the day. It's a good — not a very thick, friendship."

"But why didn't you annul the marriage?" he asked, still bewildered.

"We didn't have any need to. We had that understanding that if either of us felt the need to marry elsewhere we'd get divorced immediately. You see, we have a lot of joint property. So it involved a hassle to get divorced. I'm working, he is working; we didn't have the time or energy to spend on getting divorced."

Neil sipped his tea. "Gawd! Life can be so funny." He laughed, "And I thought I had the funniest experiences."

Cathy finished her last sip and handed the cup to Neil. He kept it on the table. She sighed and leant back on the bedpost, "Neil, I suddenly want to be like you Indians." She smiled at him, "Get married, be loved... love... and be in a Bengali family..."

He looked into her eyes. Something in his mind wanted to replace her with somebody else. He switched off the thought.

Cathy resumed her normal logical self. She waved her hand, "No really, I am serious about the proposal of you coming over. Think about it."

"I'll consider it," Neil said sincerely and held her hand.

CHAPTER 4

The Homecoming, Mahasaptami, October 16 1996

The litanies of the Mahalaya were tearing through the speakers throughout Rajdhani Express, pouring generously on the passengers, filling them up to the brim. They were all coming home. As Goddess Durga had already come into the lives and hearts of Bengal, so were they. Returning into the hearts of their own families. From various corners of the globe the Bengalis were returning home.

It was *Saptami*, the first day of the *Durga pujas*, and Neil was returning home. For the first time in two years. For the first time after Tuli's death.

The Mahalaya was piercing through his lungs. His heart. His whole existence. Why did they have to sell the album in cassettes? It was as though the entire world had conspired against him to let him know something. That he couldn't escape. To let him know that he was coming home, and that was the truth.

He felt uneasy. And was tempted to walk up to the train attendant and ask him to switch off the music. But he couldn't trust himself. He didn't know whether he would hit the man if the attendant refused. He shivered a little. He didn't know whether that was from the excess cold or something else. His mind was going numb.

He closed his eyes. He wished he could close his ears. He decided to bear the painful music. He decided to think about Cathy.

Her eyes were brimming with tears when he kissed her, bidding her goodbye at the airport. She held his hand and said, "I love you." He wished he could say the same. He simply nodded.

She said, "Just give me a ring. And I'll arrange for everything. I'm waiting for your call…" she trailed off. Her voice had cracked.

Neil felt sad for her. Sad that she was feeling so sad. He held her and hugged her close. He knew all he had to say was, "I'm coming," at that moment. But he felt tongue-tied. He simply held her. He wanted to see her happy. Cathy looked up and searched his eyes, as if trying to fathom his confusion. He smiled to hide them. But she knew. She smiled back and held his hand tight, "Don't hurry things," she said. "I'll be a friend always."

And then she turned and left. She turned back before entering the security check and waved at him, smiling. Neil too waved back. And smiled. He felt two emotions. A lump in his throat and a sense of relief. He never knew why.

He got up from the seat and walked out for a smoke. He wanted to think of Cathy and not of the place he was going to. He should have been on a plane to Stockholm and not on a train to Calcutta. He pushed the swing door of the compartment, stepped outside and lit a smoke. He had to go home someday or the other. He had to return and face his past. Good. He could think better. He opened the door of the train. Dusk sped by. Dim lights afar flashed erratically indicating that electricity had reached those villages. Before that, of course, lay acres of barren land, *aman* paddy having just been harvested.

He looked at the sky. He felt a sense of claustrophobia. Previously the sky was always his source of freedom. Now it seemed, ever since Tuli was up there, he had no escape.

Neil took a puff. He asked himself for the umpteenth time. Why was he always escaping? Why couldn't he anchor somewhere? Who was he? What was his identity? He was already twenty-four and had not started life yet. Oh yes. He's a criminal. How could he forget that? Now with that track-record it will be difficult to get a job either. He wasn't qualified enough. The only option he had was to go back and join Hassan. Join Juhi. Perhaps even marry her. That was the only way out. Or get a job through her. Then of course, he'd have to marry her. He felt uneasy. Sick. Claustrophobic. Felt as if someone was throttling him. He simply had to try for a visa. He had to go to Stockholm. That was his only option.

He threw the cigarette on the speeding tracks and went inside. He looked at the happy faces. The happy families who were all going back home on holidays. They'd meet their relatives and all would be so happy. He sat down. When did he last feel *happy*? He didn't remember. What was happiness? Was he searching for happiness or *searching for an escape from it?*

He didn't have an answer. His eyes stung with self-pity. He decided to sleep. *He decided never to wake up...*

CHAPTER 5

Calcutta, Mahashtami, October 17 1996

The taxi came to a halt. That lane. That by-lane where the ruffians were hiding to beat him up. He got off from the taxi and started walking. He looked into the lane. A foot-wide lane. A typical characteristic feature of central Calcutta with century-old houses crammed up on either side. He had played with his friends so many times in these lanes.

Then he looked up at the house. He could hear the drums beating. It was another *Ashtami* morning and the house should be teeming with his relatives. Nobody knew he was coming. He thought of sneaking in upstairs.

Mahamaya spotted him first.

"Neilu!" she shrieked above the sound of the drums and came rushing down the *thakurdalan* throwing whatever she had in her hands. Everybody turned. In an instant there was a small crowd around him. Sujoy was hugging his waist, Mahamaya his neck. His father was patting his back. His uncles and aunts asking in different tones, "Where were you?… Why didn't you write for so long?… Why didn't you inform you were coming?… Leave him alone… he's tired. Neilu come upstairs…" The drummer stopped playing for a moment not knowing whether he should go on. Somebody scolded him and he resumed the beats.

His mother held his hand and led him upstairs. "You must be hungry, I'll cook *luchi* [41] for you." *Luchi* had been his all time favorites.

"No Mom, I've had breakfast on the train…" His protest got lost in the clamor.

"Where *were* you?" Mahamaya suddenly reached the top of the stairs and broke down. "…We were all so worried. We received only two letters from you and sent repeated letters at that address. We rang up repeatedly. The phone kept on ringing. We were thinking of informing the police…" She broke down and wiped her eyes with her new red-bordered white *sari*.

Neil had never seen her breaking down like that ever in his life. He put an arm around her to comfort her. It was so overwhelming. He never had felt so wanted in his whole life. He felt happy. So? This was happiness?

Mahamaya led him in to the dining hall. The small crowd followed. He was so overwhelmed he couldn't speak a word. He simply held Sujoy's hand and hugged his mom. He felt Neepa and his aunts trailing behind him and his father walking by his side.

He entered the hall. *And then it struck him.*

The same smiling face laughing at everybody. Tuli's photograph. Adorned with fresh garlands. Hung on the wall opposite the entrance. He stopped on his tracks. He wanted to flee. *No!* This wasn't happening to him! This wasn't his house! He couldn't stay here!

He turned to walk out of the room. Mahamaya held his hand, "Won't you eat?"

"No," he pushed the crowd aside and ran. He leapt up the stairs to his room, as if something was chasing him.

Mahamaya quickly called out, "Manik, run! Open Chhorda's room. It's locked. Go fast!"

She knew her son's moods. Suddenly he might just turn and walk out of the house, *never to return again.* She turned and looked at Tuli's photograph. She found herself thinking of removing the picture from there.

Neil stepped onto the terrace. It was a pleasant, sunny day. The sky was blue and white autumn clouds sailed by…. *The sky became overcast… white streaks of lightning slashed across…a hurricane blew haywire... Tuli's orange sari was flying in the wind like a raging wildfire... she looked so peaceful...*

Neil clenched his fist and closed his eyes. He opened them and saw the calm, sunny morning.

He walked towards his room. Manik ran past him suddenly with the key. He noticed his room had been locked. The obedient servant opened the lock and then the door. He smiled at him, "I'll bring some tea," he said and left.

Neil walked into his room. It was clean, but uninhabited. The bedspread was spic and span. The computer was well covered. His cupboard was locked. The floor was clean. The room smelt alien... unfamiliar... cold... unwelcoming...

He sat on the bed and let his palm run over the bedspread... *Tuli giggled beneath his hands... and jumped up and hugged him... wearing just her sindoor smeared across her forehead... her hair wild over her face... "I love you, stupid. Where were you all these days?"...*

"Chhorda, tea." Neil jumped and looked at Manik standing at the door. He left the tea on the computer table. Manik saw something in his eyes he would never forget. He came out and wiped his eyes.

Neil looked down at the empty bed. He walked over and sipped the tea. Which part of the house should he go to now? Where can he escape his pain?

He took the cup of tea and walked down the terrace by the back stairs. He went into Mahamaya's room.

He had to phone somebody. His friends in Calcutta. He placed the teacup on the table wondering where he had last kept his phonebook. The drums had stopped playing.

Mahamaya came inside.

"Neilu, come, sit. I want to speak to you." She sat on the bed.

He numbly followed her instructions and sat on the bed beside her. She held his hand. "Where are you working in Mumbai?"

"Huh..?" Neil looked up. And crossed his brows. He tried to remember. "Barry's Travel Agency." He said without thinking.

"Where are you staying? At the same place?"

He shook his head. He didn't like Mahamaya holding his hand and released it in the pretext of sipping his tea.

"What happened to you? Neilu, I'm your mother. I gave birth to you. Can't you confide in me?"

He had a terrible urge to say 'Thanks', but simply said, "Nothing."

Mahamaya decided to try another access. "You know, your father has lost a lot of money in business. Somu couldn't handle it properly. A lot of money was lost. Now he is being hounded by creditors."

Neil understood her. It's the age-old method in Bengali families to show your weaknesses to your children once they are grown up, so that you could haul them back. So they became responsible and contributed to the family's income. He understood the trust she was placing in her. He understood the trust she had lost in her elder son. *He wanted to say he wasn't there at all…*

Mahamaya was speaking, "Somu is spending a lot of money wildly on bad company. Your father is very upset. Neilu, you know, I have a plan. I want to get him married again. This time with a city girl…"

The words hit him like a splash of ice water. He gulped his hot tea down.

"….You know how much he had loved your *boudi*. I've found a girl who's almost as beautiful. But more educated."

Neil stood up. And walked out.

"Where are you going?"

He didn't answer.

He met Sujoy standing against the railings. He had grown a few inches taller. Neil smiled at him. He cast his eyes down.

Neil came near him and held his face up, "Hmm… another few inches and you'd catch me."

Sujoy suddenly hugged him and burst out crying. He shook with the sob. Neil had the cup of tea in his hands and so he couldn't hug him back.

"Hey… guys don't cry. Didn't you learn that? Guys are not supposed to cry. You are a man."

He pulled back. His eyes were smeared with tears. He looked down at the courtyard. The *Ashtami puja aaroti* was over and devotees were standing with marigold, hibiscus flowers and *bael* leaves in their hands, chanting mantra after the priest, waiting to offer the flowers and leaves at the goddess's feet. They were offering *anjali* [40].

"You didn't offer *anjali*?" Neil asked. Sujoy remained silent. He pressed his lips and opened his closed palm. There was a piece of dry hibiscus and a *bael* leaf. "She gave me this… two years back. I've never given *anjali* after that…"

Neil kept the cup on the floor and pulled him to hug him. The two men hugged each other and let tears roll silently down their cheeks — loving one woman in two different ways — feeling the pain together — killing the pain together — reinstating Tuli's wiped out existence in their air.

The anjali was over.

CHAPTER 6

Hodolchua, October 18 1996

Hodolchua is no living thing. It's a village.

Twenty kilometers off-route Jhargram, a town in West Bengal. It's a seven-hour drive from Calcutta. It's no earthshakingly beautiful spot. In fact, it's no tourist spot at all. There were no tourist bungalows or hotels. Civilization ceased within a few minutes of leaving Jhargram. Dry patches of barren land, red, sandy, unfriendly soil, devoid of any cultivation, spread wide along the two sides of the highway.

Beyond that tamarisk, *mahua,* [42] *palash* [43] and cotton forests climbed up short hills. In fact, the highway vanished quite quickly and a stretch of red, muddy road rolled out in front of your vehicle. A wild smoke of red dust followed the wheels. Sporadic sets of mud huts adorned with extensive hand paintings, emerged and vanished without warning.

The dusky, yet shiny aboriginal women, called *Santhals,* [44] wearing red-bordered white cotton *saris* without any blouse or petticoat, looked at you as perplexed as you were on seeing them. Completely nude children stared at your vehicle, which is as frequent on their roads as is a flying saucer in a city. Their fastest mode of transportation was the bullock cart — which they availed only when they had to carry their harvest to the town dealers. They were mostly used to their own vehicles. Their legs. Which carried them for miles without much effort.

The women were more active than the men. They carried long, chopped wood from the forest on their heads and walked along the dusty road for kilometers to the markets, early in the mornings. Whatever money they earned from that, they bought their daily intake of rice, pulses and vegetables and walked back home. Then they cooked their food — their first meal of the day. In the evenings they dressed up — which included abundantly adorning their hair with red *palash* flowers. Then they drank *mahua* and danced to the beats of a *madol* [45]. The *Santhal* dance is an exquisite form of art that had enthralled the world forever.

A set of women attired in a blend of red and white *sari*, stark against their jet black varnished skin and large black eyes, held each other by the waist and swayed together, taking small steps to the intoxicating rhythm of their typical song — rivetingly attuned to the pulsating rhythm of the *madol*.

The *madol* is played mostly by the tribal men. They were less active of the two genders. Their activities comprised extracting a drink from the *mahua* flowers, helping the women in cutting trees and lending a hand in the household chores.

The *mahua* flowers were typical of Bengal and smelt of fine quality Basmati rice. Its wonderful smell attracted bears — available in abundance in the forests — which climbed down the hills during spring to drink the juice from it. The swishing tamarisk forests also housed a few more wild animals like boars and jackals.

Neil winced in the afternoon sun, which had reflected itself on the red soil, making the world look amber. He wished he had brought his pair of sunglasses. Ambik had recited the list to him over the phone. He simply had nodded. And then when he had put down the receiver, he only remembered a 'torch' and a 'stick'. He tried to remember the name of the place. Hodol... something. The trip sounded exciting. A wild adventure into the forest! Ambik, Harris and Pillai were camping there for two nights and three days. He had luckily called Remo's flat in Calcutta and got Ambik.

"Hey! When did you come to Calcutta?"

"Just today." The gang in Calcutta knew nothing of Remo's imprisonment. Neil decided not to tell them anything.

"Tomorrow we're going camping to Hodolchua. Wanna go?"

"Where?"

"Hodolchua. It's off Jhargram."

"Who found the place?"

"Pillai. You remember Pillai? That Southy in Math Honors?"

"Oh, yes. Where are you going to stay?"

"We're camping. We're taking tents and cooking stuff. Just take a plate, a torch, sunglasses, cap, walking shoes, candles and a stick."

"A stick?"

"Yes, man. We're staying inside the forest. If a bear comes along, at least we can beat him up. Ha! Ha!"

Neil pondered a while. "Where do we meet?"

"Great, so you'll come. We'll pick you up."

"No." He didn't want anybody to know where he was going. "I'll come over to Alipore. When are you guys leaving?"

"We have Harris' Sumo. You know he's bought a Sumo; rather it's his father's. We'll leave by eight."

"Fine, I'll be there."

⇉⇇

"Hey," said Ambik, sitting at the driving wheel. "Come back."

"Huh...?" Neil turned. And smiled.

"How was Bombay?"

"Fine," Neil quickly said.

"You're working?"

"Yah." Neil didn't like the probing. He looked behind him. Pillai and Harris swayed their heads to the music of the latest remix of old Hindi songs being played on the car deck. The Tata Sumo car was speeding at 60km per hour.

"So what are you guys up to?" he asked smiling.

"India is drab," quipped Harris. "There's nothing to do out here. I'll leave."

"Really? Where do you plan to go?"

"London. My aunt's sponsoring me."

"That's great. What about you, Pillai?"

"I'm working for a courier company. A sales executive."

With Math? As far as Neil remembered, Pillai had topped the class in one of the pre-tests. He felt the same sense of claustrophobia.

He wanted to smash the window-screen with his fists. He turned away.

Harris spoke, as if he read Neil's mind. "You are with a travel agent, aren't you Neil?" He laughed, "Just imagine the state of this country. We're a bunch from Presidency — toppers in English, Math and History — and we land up in jobs in sales with peanut salaries. Gawd! We should have had a Sales Honours in our education system."

They all laughed. They all felt piercing pain within.

CHAPTER 7

Neil Must Die

Neil must die. Somebody up there was making sure of it. It wasn't as if he chose his death. He chose to live. To survive in the madness as an honest, upright human being. But the more he escaped from death, the more it seemed to follow him.

He died several deaths. It began with leaving Tuli. Something died in him when he left her. Then he died, when she died. He died when he joined Hassan. He died when they cornered his only friend he had in his life — Remo. He died when Cathy left and he realized he didn't love her. He died again when he saw that though he was forgiven wholeheartedly by his family members, Tuli's existence was getting wiped out from the Roy household. But mostly, he died the same day somebody told him, *"The 'baby' was dead already"*.

He had died several times. He should have died on that day when Soumen's men beat him up. But he survived that only to die several deaths after that. He was already a dead man. A dead man escaping death. Despite that, somebody up there showed no mercy on him. He must die. His physical self must die. Neil wondered why hadn't he committed suicide? To make things easier for God. He wondered why was he escaping? He should just stand at one point and let fate annihilate him completely.

The cool breeze was consolingly refreshing. He hated it. He hated the pity that Hodolchua was bestowing on him. Hodolchua was being kind to him. Very kind. The beautiful, calm forest, the wonderful moonlight and the swishing tamarisk breeze made him feel that there were so many more beautiful things in life. He hated to hope. He hated the hope Hodolchua was trying to restore in him. He knew he'd be back in civilization a day later. He had only one more night. He hated the peace that he felt within him.

It should be past midnight. Ambik, Harris and Pillai were snoring in the tent. Neil lay flat on the grass looking at the moon. Three cigarettes lay annihilated around him. He didn't feel like smoking anymore. There was a ring of fire on top of a hill in front of him. He didn't know why it was there. He wondered if the fire would come down and burn him finally.

And then he heard it!

Faintly at first. Then the beats came in louder. They sailed through the breeze and sent a pulsating rhythm into his soul. He recognized the instrument. *Madol*. There must be a celebration at a nearby *Santhal* village.

He stood up. He didn't have a torch. He didn't care. The moonlight was there. He began walking towards the rhythm.

He walked for almost a kilometer before he heard the *madol* filling up the air completely. And then he saw them.

Down from the path on which he was standing, a few mud huts stood still in the moonlight. A fire was burning high at the center. He clambered downhill towards them. A few *Santhal* women in red-bordered white *saris* were dancing around the fire. Giggling — their white teeth stark against their varnished black skin. Two men, sitting on their haunches, were playing the *madols*. A group of men and women were sitting at a corner and drinking.

They spotted him. They were all stone-drunk and laughed at him. Neil felt they were doing the right thing. Laughing at him. He too laughed and walked over to the group. He sat down and asked for a drink.

"Hey! *Sahab* has come. Hey, give him a drink. *Sahab* you have put up tents out there, haven't you?"

"Yes," Neil smiled. He felt a surprising relaxation. He took a drink in an earthen pot. He brought it near his lips. It smelt strong. He gulped down the liquid. It left a sweet, tingly aftertaste. He liked it. He held out the pot for more.

"Hey, give *Sahab* more. *Sahab*, you're married?"

Neil smiled, "No."

"*Sahab*, don't marry *Sahab*," the man laughed. "Marriage spoils everything."

Neil looked at him perplexed. The man laughed and fell back. He supported himself with his hands and sat up. A dark girl brought Neil another drink. She had no blouse and her firm breasts were hanging against the cotton *sari*. Her eyes were large and innocent. He looked at her and then took the drink. She immediately giggled and ran off. Neil laughed too. He didn't know why he laughed. He drank the liquid, again in one gulp.

He held out the pot, "No more," he shook his head.

"No *Sahab*, have one more. Hey, Bijli, give *Sahab* another."

The same girl came in front of him. She leant forward and knelt down. Neil looked at her large eyes. He remembered *he had loved those eyes*. But this was Bijli. *How can she have the same eyes?*

She smiled and handed him the drink. Neil took the pot and kept looking at those eyes. She burst out giggling. Then she ran and joined the women dancing around the fire.

The drumbeats had reached a crescendo and were building up an orgasm through the cells. Neil drank the liquid. He drank another. And then another. The dancers were now gyrating wildly. In fact the entire world was swaying wildly. The drummers too were jumping and dancing to the intoxicating cadence that was saturating the air.

Bijli now danced in the center. Her whole body was wild. Her hands were free and unrestrained. Once in the air, once behind her head, once behind her back. The licking flames turned her into an amber-colored passion. Neil wanted to hold her, touch her, have wild sex with her, rolling on the grass.

Bijli circled around the fire and then she came around, she was not Bijli! *She was Tuli!* She had become fair and beautiful. Large eyes, long neck, no blouse, her breasts firmly bouncing against her white *sari*. Tuli was laughing and calling Neil. She waved at him and asked him to join her. Neil laughed and closed his eyes. Tuli was dead. This was another of his hallucinations. Or was it? Was he dead too? Maybe he was. He didn't care. He opened his eyes. He saw a small figure had joined the group. A small boy, completely nude, was wearing just a red *palash* flower garland around his neck. He was dancing too. He was Aakash. Neil knew it. The same curly black hair, like his. The same big eyes like Tuli's.

He stood up. Tuli was beckoning him with her hand. He laughed and staggered towards her. Tuli left the dancing group and started walking. She was laughing and began running. She was drunk and staggered. Neil started to run, but found his legs were very heavy. He was trying to catch her. But she was way off. He remembered Aakash and turned. He didn't see him. Maybe they had taken him inside. He looked ahead. Tuli had vanished among the trees!

He ran towards the trees. The path was a steep climb and Tuli was nowhere. He called out, "Tuli, Tuli, don't play with me... I love you... I want you, Tuli. Please come back."

And then he saw her. She was standing on top of the hill. Beyond the tamarisk trees. Neil laughed when he saw her. And began climbing. She kept giggling. Neil reached the top and held out his hand to catch her. She ducked. And then she was nowhere!

Neil looked below. The world was looking so wonderful, so far, down below. He felt his foot slipping and his head hit hard against something. His hands tried to grope for a bush, but slipped. And then he felt air. Air all around him until his head hit something very hard. He knew he had fallen off the cliff. He was dead. He was finally dead. He was finally free. He wanted to get up. He knew he wouldn't die. He would survive again. But he felt sleep paralyzing him. He let his soul rest...

He slept...

The tamarisk trees swayed lightly in the breeze. A crow cawed. It was dawn.

CONCLUSION

Whether Neil dies in the end is your choice. If he lives, *you* made him live. If he dies, it's *you* who decides. Honestly, I couldn't come to a decision. I didn't have the heart to let him die the way I let Tuli die. And couldn't let him live on and suffer more, since there was nothing more he could live on for.

I hated myself for letting Tuli die and often, very often, thought of bringing her back to life… somehow… But the harsh reality of life got in my way.

I apprehend my readers would essentially be categorized in two groups: One who would instantly relate to the characters and situations. And the other, who would understand the characters impersonally. It's the second group of readers I am looking forward to for critical quips. Since the first group would be too emotional to give an impartial view. However, I invite any comments from you on my website.

This novel, I presumed, helped readers learn a lot about India and the reality of its culture and urban lives. Though the events take place some years before India actually went through a communication reincarnation — when cell phones, computers and internet took over the common lives of Indians — I guess you do know now that India exists beyond kings, snakes, elephants and chicken *tikka masala*! And that India is not just a *poor* country. It also has riches beyond imaginations. Often inside unhealthy pockets.

And as for the real critics, well, you are on the seat of judgment! And I *am* scared!

Kaberi Chatterjee

Glossary of terms

1. *Mahalaya: Mahisasura Mardini* (The Annihilation of the Demon) is a hugely popular radio program that is broadcasted on the new moon day prior to the Durga Puja, a day which is also known as *Mahalaya*. Since 1930, this program has been aired on All India Radio (AIR). It is a two-and-a-half hour audio montage of chanting Sanskrit *slokas*, Bengali devotional songs, classical music with a dash of acoustic melodrama. The program begins at 4 am and ends at dawn, and inspires entire Bengal to wake up and listen to the devotional deluge even today.

2. *Babuji:* Addressing a man with respect.

3. *Durga Puja:* The biggest festival in India, particularly Bengal, held at the advent of autumn or fall where the Goddess of strength and harmony is worshipped for four days. (Refer to 1.) It is the most colorful occasion for the people when they forget all their animosity and unhappiness to unite for the frenzied festival. This celebration is the annual and final one of the Bengalis and marked the advent of peace and harmony in their land. Millions of rupees are spend to construct temporary puja sites, called, *pandals*. The *pandals* and the idols of Durga are hailed as works of art. Thousands from all over the world visit these *pandals* just to see the handicraft. However, this beauty lasts just for four days after which the idols are immersed in River Ganges and the pandals pulled down.

4. *Maduli:* India is a blend of the extreme ancient and extreme modernism. On one hand India has the top

technologists, doctors and engineers of the world and on the other, common people still holds immense faith in astrologers, exorcists and spiritual healers. Hence, along with possessing the best education, availing the best technology, these people take their final advice from their personal astrologers or exorcists, who give them spiritual flowers encased inside small metal cubes, which they hang from their arms tied to fat strings.

5. *Bindi:* Small, round, colored adornments, worn on foreheads.

6. *Thakurdalan:* Elaborately ornamented elevated platform with pillars and baroque arches overlooking a courtyard in a stately house in Bengal. This platform is essentially kept holy and empty for worshipping the *Durga Puja* once a year. Possessing a *thakurdalan* in Bengal is an ultimate status quo.

7. *Mithais:* Indian sweets made with milk and various other ingredients. Ghee is extensively used in making *mithais*.

8. *Ghee:* Homemade butter made from frozen cream.

9. *Bidi:* Cheaply made cigarettes from inferior ingredients and has been the smoking choice for the poor in India. Called 'the poor man's cigarette', the *bidi* is made from the flakes and dust of dark tobacco leaves. This concoction is then hand-rolled in tamarisk leaves. The unfiltered final product is a small, slim cigarette, tied at both ends with a colored thread.

10. *Bhatiali:* Originally from Bangladesh and West Bengal in India, they are songs expressing the simple joys and sorrows of the lives of boatmen.

11. *Dada:* Elder brother.

12. *Anchal:* Lose end of the sari that dangles from the back of a woman's shoulder.

13. *Dharmashalas:* Inns or motels near holy places.

14. *Gurdwar:* Holy place of worship for the Sikhs.

15. *Paisa:* Indian money, change.

16. *Puri:* Small balls of kneaded flour rolled out and deep-fried in hot oil.

17. *Alu-bhaji:* Spicy potato fries.

18. *Rabindrasangeet:* Also known as Tagore Songs in English, is a form of music composed by Nobel Laureate Rabindranath Tagore, who added a new dimension to the musical concept of India in general and Bengal in specific. *Rabindrasangeet* use Indian classical music and traditional folk music as sources. Tagore wrote some 2,230 songs. The Rabindrasangeet, which deal with varied themes are immensely popular and form a foundation for the Bengali ethos that is comparable to, perhaps even greater than, that which Shakespeare has on the English-speaking world. It is said that his songs are the outcome of 500 years of literary and cultural churning that the Bengali community has gone through.

19. *Khichri:* A Bengali concoction of rice and pulses cooked with ghee, vegetables and spices.

20. *Gotra:* A *gotra* is the lineage or clan assigned to a Hindu at birth. In most cases, the system is patri-lineal and the *gotra* assigned is that of the person's father. Other terms for it are *vansh, vanshaj, bedagu, purvik, purvajan, pitru*. An individual may decide to identify his lineage by a different *gotra*, or combination of *gotras*.

21. *Phulsojya:* The night of conjugation for newly-wed couples, two days after the actual marriage ceremony.

22. *Chowbachcha:* Tank of water inside a residential house which is connected to the main city water pipeline from which municipality water rushes in at specific times.

23. *Kajal: Kohl; suruma;* is a mixture of soot and ghee used predominantly by women in the Middle East, South Asia, North Africa and the Horn of Africa to darken the eyelids and as mascara for the their eyelashes. It is also sometimes spelled *kol, kehal* or *kohal* in the Arab world and is known as *surma* or *kajal* in South Asia. Kohl has been worn traditionally as far back as the Bronze Age (3500 B.C. onward) by the Egyptian queens. It was originally

used as protection against eye ailments. There was also a belief that darkening around the eyes would protect one from the harsh rays of the sun. India's oldest caste, the *koli*, used kohl as a cosmetic. In addition, mothers would apply kohl to their infants' eyes soon after birth. Some did this to "strengthen the child's eyes", and others believed it could prevent the child from being cursed by the evil eye.

24. *Didi*: Addressing a young girl with respect.

25. *Boudi*: Addressing one's elder brother's wife with respect.

26. *Roak*: Elevated platform at the main entrance of stately houses in India. This is a specialty in Bengal and is a venue for warm winter afternoon chats, evening discussions or simple gossip. *Roak* is a structural liberty in a Bengali household that speaks of its unhurried lifestyle and has often been the seed of its intellectual feats. However, with the newest surge in buildings and high-rises, *roaks* are vanishing fast, though it continues to adorn a few houses in cities like Calcutta and a few suburban towns.

27. *Durwan*: Doorman, security guard.

28. *Satyanarayan Puja*: Worshipping God Narayana, supreme Hindu god. Some superstitious Bengalis believe that worshipping Narayana or Vishnu at a troubled juncture in their lives would waiver off the issue instantly.

29. *Ojha*: Exorcist.

30. *Supari*: Code used by the Mumbai underworld to express money taken to commit a murder.

31. *Dhaba*: Small hotels which serve meals.

32. *Randi*: Prostitute, whore.

33. *Dhoti*: White yards of cloth worn by Indian men to mark an occasion or celebration.

34. *Kurta*: Loose t-shirt worn over *dhoti* or pajama.

35. *Aaroti* : During a *puja*, the priest wounds a set of burning lamps in air in front of the deity to hail the deity in the daily lives of the devotees.

36. *Rumali roti:* Hand-made paper-thin chapattis made out of white flour.

37. *Tadka:* Tasty tempered lentils cooked in spice.

38. *Sindoor:* Sindoor is a red powder (Vermilion), which is traditionally applied along the parting-line of a woman's hair (also called *mang*) or as a dot on the forehead. *Sindoor* is the mark of a married woman in Hinduism. Single women wear the dot in different colors (*bindi* in Hindi) but do not apply *sindoor* in their *mang*. Hindu widows do not wear the *sindoor*, signifying that their husband is no longer alive.

39. *Ghat:* Hindu burial ground where pyres are lit.

40. *Dom:* The *Domba* or *Dom* (Sanskrit *doma*, dialectally also *Domaki, Dombo, Domra, Domaka, Dombar* and variants) are an ethnic or social group, or groups, scattered across India. They are usually segregated from the mainstream community as outcastes. The *Domba* are sometimes also called *Chandala*. Both terms also came to be used in the sense of 'outcaste' in general. People identified as *Doms* have long been workers at cremation places, scavengers, or weavers of ropes and baskets.

41. *Chandan:* Sandalwood paste, considered holy in Hindu rites.

42. *Anjali:* A ritual during worshipping a deity when devotees hold flowers and bael leaves in their hands and chant *mantra* (Sanskrit hymns) after which they offer the flowers to the deity.

43. *Luchi:* Rolled-out small and round flour balls deep fried in oil.

44. *Mahua:* (Wikipedia) *Madhuca longifolia*, commonly known as *mahwa* or *mahua*, is an Indian tropical tree found largely in the central and north Indian plains and forests. It is adapted to arid environments, being a prominent tree in tropical mixed deciduous forests in India in the states of Jharkhand, Uttar Pradesh, Bihar, Madhya Pradesh, Kerala, Gujarat and Orissa. The flowers of *mahua* tree are fermented to produce an alcoholic drink called *mahua*,

a country liquor. Tribals of Bastar in Chattisgarh and Orissa, Santhals of Santhal Paraganas (Jharkhand) and Tribals of North Maharashtra, consider the tree and the *mahua* drink as part of their cultural heritage. Tribal people, men and women, consume this drink and is an obligatory item during celebrations and evening activities. [5] The main ingredients used for making *mahua* are the *chhowa gud* (mollasses in granular form) and dried *mahua* flowers.

45. *Palash:* A red seasonal flower which aborigines like Santhals use to adorn their hair.

46. *Santhal:* With a population of more than 49000, Santhal tribes are the third largest tribes in India. Belonging to pre-Aryan period, these tribes of India are found in regions of West Bengal, Bihar, Orissa and Jharkhand.

47. *Madol* : An elongated percussion instrument that is particularly played by the men of the Santhal tribes.